"There's Nothing Humiliating About Wanting A Man—

Even a man like me."

His self-deprecating statement startled her. "Nick, what happened last night had nothing to do with you."

Slowly it dawned on Cecily that Nick had taken her around Glenville, shown her the scenes of his past, given her a tour not of the town but of himself and his life. Apparently he thought she'd rejected him last night out of snobbishness. "Nick what happened last night was. . ." She drifted off uncertainly.

"You wanted me," he supplied for her.

"Yes. But I don't even know you. My husband—I knew him for months and months before I ever felt. . ."

"Before you ever felt what you felt for me last night?"

"Yes," she whispered.

Dear Reader,

Welcome to Silhouette! Our goal is to give you hours of unbeatable reading pleasure, and we hope you'll enjoy each month's six new Silhouette Desires. These sensual, provocative love stories are both believable and compelling—sometimes they're poignant, sometimes humorous, but always enjoyable.

Indulge yourself. Experience all the passion and excitement of falling in love along with our heroine as she meets the irresistible man of her dreams and together they overcome all obstacles in the path to a happy ending.

If this is your first Desire, I hope it'll be the first of many. If you're already a Silhouette Desire reader, thanks for your support! Look for some of your favorite authors in the coming months: Stephanie James, Diana Palmer, Dixie Browning, Ann Major and Doreen Owens Malek, to name just a few.

Happy reading!

Isabel Swift
Senior Editor

ARIEL BERK
Teacher's Pet

Silhouette Desire

Published by Silhouette Books New York

America's Publisher of Contemporary Romance

SILHOUETTE BOOKS
300 E. 42nd St., New York, N.Y. 10017

Copyright © 1985 by Barbara Keiler

Distributed by Pocket Books

ISBN: 0-373-05250-2

First Silhouette Books printing December 1985

10 9 8 7 6 5 4 3 2 1

Printed in the U.S.A.

Books by Ariel Berk

Silhouette Desire

ARIEL BERK

is not only a novelist, she is a composer. In her spare time she enjoys activities as disparate as sailing, sunbathing, hiking and visiting museums, but she lets nothing take too much time away from her pleasure in writing.

One

Just as Cecily feared: Richard Pettibone was waiting for her after the final bell. He loitered in the hallway some ten feet from her classroom door, fidgeting with a locker handle and pretending not to be watching for her to leave. She stepped out of the room, her leather portfolio in one hand, an open carton containing student essays tucked beneath the other arm, and her keys clenched in her teeth. As soon as she entered the corridor and heaved the door shut with her hip, he sprang to attention.

"Hey, Mrs. Adams." He loped to her side and reached for the carton. "Let me lend you a hand."

Given that she hadn't yet mastered the trick of locking a door with her mouth, she reluctantly let him take the carton. "Thank you, Richard," she said with forced politeness after she'd removed the keys from her mouth and locked the door.

He really was becoming a pest, and she wasn't quite sure how to deal with him. A tall, gangly boy, slightly underweight, with an unkempt shock of straw-colored hair, Richard possessed an eager attentiveness that Cecily had initially welcomed. He was shy but obviously intelligent, and she wanted to encourage his interest in her government systems course. So she'd let him stay after class to erase the blackboards, close the blinds and ask endless questions about the homework. But now, one month into the fall term, she was beginning to regret her friendliness. The teenager was clearly smitten with her, and she couldn't think of a tactful way to tell him to cool off and leave her alone.

"This box is awfully heavy," he remarked as she slipped her key ring into the pocket of her tweed blazer and then reached for the carton. "Let me carry it outside for you."

"No, Richard, that's all right, I can manage it."

"I'll carry it out for you," he insisted, turning from her and lugging the carton toward the stairwell at the end of the hall.

Cecily pressed her lips together in annoyance as she followed him to the stairs. How did one tell an earnest sixteen-year-old boy with hang-dog eyes and a fragile ego that he ought to stick to girls his own age? If Cecily so much as hinted that she knew Richard had a crush on her, she'd sound terribly presumptuous, and she'd wind up embarrassing them both.

It was an alien situation for her, even though she knew she was reasonably attractive. She'd been graced with a tall, slender build, and her hair fell just past her shoulders in lustrous auburn waves. Her features were delicate, with widely set green eyes, an even, narrow nose and a warm, dimpled smile. If not breathtaking, her looks were certainly more than moderately appealing. She also knew she appeared younger than her thirty years, even in the conservative clothing she deliberately wore to give her an aura of authority. But a high-school junior ought to be escorting some girl his own age from the school, not his teacher.

Nothing like this had ever occurred during her previous job—but then, it wouldn't have. Within a month after starting work at the well-maintained high school in one of Long Island's more upper-crust towns, Cecily had begun to date the school's bachelor football coach, and by the end of the school year she and Phil were married. Not surprisingly, they were kidded a great deal about their marital status, nicknamed "The Adams Family" and subjected to loud kissing noises from the students whenever they were seen chatting in one of the hallways. But nobody had ever hounded either of them the way Richard was hounding Cecily now.

Following him down the stairs, Cecily recalled her conversation with Gary Czymanski in the faculty lounge earlier that day. Blond and well-built, Gary would presumably have to fend off the attentions of giggly female students; Cecily thought her fellow social studies teacher might have some advice for her regarding Richard. "Forgive me, Gary," she'd said, settling herself beside him on one of the vinyl sofas in the gloomy lounge, "but have any of your students ever had crushes on you? I mean, you're a good-looking guy, and—"

Gary had tossed back his head with a laugh. "Am I supposed to forgive you for complimenting me?" He'd jammed out his cigarette and reached for his coffee. "Why do you ask? Has some kid gone soft for you?"

She'd nodded dolefully. "I can't think of a diplomatic way to call him off, Gary. How do you handle these things?"

Gary had studied her for a long moment, then laughed again. "To tell the truth, Cecily, it doesn't happen to me. I always take preemptive measures. The very first day of class, I find some way to mention my wife. Every chance I get, I refer to her. I lecture on Debbie's opinion of the Battle of Hastings, Debbie's thoughts about the Thirty Years' War— you name it, I get Debbie into the discussion. I also wave my left hand in the air a lot," he'd added, demonstrating for Cecily by flashing his wedding band beneath her nose.

Cecily had smiled slightly. "I don't suppose that'll work for me," she'd commented wryly.

Gary's grin had abruptly faded. "Oh, Cecily, I'm sorry," he'd muttered.

She'd cringed but managed a chuckle. She despised the way pity seemed to color her relationships with her friends and colleagues, even here in Glenville, hundreds of miles from Long Island. "Don't be sorry," she'd chided Gary gently. "Just give me some suggestions about how to get Richard Pettibone out of my hair."

Gary had mulled over her options. "I don't suppose you could invent a husband," he'd mused. "Maybe a boyfriend. You could pretend you're already attached and sneak the news into your conversations with the kid. Maybe he'll take the hint."

Keeping pace with Richard as they approached the door leading outside to the faculty parking lot, Cecily mulled over Gary's recommendation and scowled. How could she pretend she had a boyfriend? She'd been living in Glenville only a couple of months. Besides, she wasn't good at play-acting. Creating an imaginary boyfriend wasn't the sort of thing Cecily would be able to do with much conviction.

Richard held the door open for her, and they exited the building. Glenville High School showed its age; a stodgy three-story brownstone structure, it was long past its prime. The classrooms were sorely in need of fresh paint; the lockers were rusted; the library was desperately short of books.

But the city of Glenville was suffering more than enough financial crises at the moment, and renovating the high school wasn't the top priority.

As she strolled along the crumbling concrete walk that led to the parking lot, she tried to ignore the dewy-eyed looks Richard kept tossing her way. She drew to a halt at the edge of the lot and forced another courteous smile. "Thanks for your assistance, Richard," she said as she tried once more to take the box of student essays from him.

"Where's your car, Mrs. Adams?" he asked, resolutely refusing to hand her the box. "This is heavy—I'll carry it to the car for you."

"Really, Richard, I can handle it," she countered, wedging her portfolio under her arm and tugging at the box.

He stubbornly twisted away from her, and a brisk gust of wind lifted several papers from the open top of the box. "Uh-oh," he grunted, dropping the box to chase the drifting pages. The box landed on its side and more papers tumbled out.

Stifling a curse, Cecily set the box upright on the curb and then darted across the lot, trying to gather the wind-strewn papers. "Damn Richard for being such an insufferable gentleman," she grumbled, the stack heels of her leather pumps clicking against the asphalt and the wind ruffling the hem of her pleated woolen skirt. Scooping up several papers that had gotten caught beneath the tire of a parked car, she banged her knuckles against the coarse pavement and cursed again.

Adding the papers to the small stack she'd retrieved, she stood and noticed a man collecting several stray sheets of paper that the breeze had pinned to the chain link fence separating the parking lot from the school's athletic field. Clad in jeans and a dark leather jacket, the man had apparently been watching the football team's practice ses-

sion. He sorted the papers into a neat pile and turned to
Cecily.

His hair was thick and black, swept back from his high
brow by the invigorating autumn wind. His eyes were nearly
as dark as his hair, his skin a deep bronze. He had a prom-
inent nose, a firm, angular jaw and an enticing smile that
expanded as his gaze fastened onto Cecily.

She started across the lot to him. He appeared about to
speak, but suddenly Richard galloped toward him from the
far end of the lot shouting, "Hey, mister, I'll get those!"

Pretend you're attached, Cecily contemplated, remembering Gary's advice. From the corner of her eye she saw
Richard rapidly approaching, anxious to collect the papers
from the dark-haired, dark-eyed man and present himself as
Cecily's hero. Now was her chance, if she was impulsive
enough to dare....

"Sweetheart!" she cried out, dashing to the dark man and
flinging her arms flamboyantly around his broad shoulders. "What a surprise!"

One of the man's eyebrows quirked upward, but he didn't
shrink from her. "What a surprise is right," he mumbled,
glancing toward Richard.

Cecily glanced toward the boy as well, and then spun back
to the stranger she'd just cast in the role of her imaginary
boyfriend. She wanted to explain to him what she was
doing, but Richard was almost upon them. Her eyes pleaded
with the man not to give her away, and he winked.

Gasping for breath, Richard drew to a halt beside them,
clutching the box and a mess of papers. He panted as his
vision traveled from Cecily to the stranger and back again.
The man slid his arm around Cecily's narrow waist and held
her snugly to himself. Richard's eyes narrowed suspiciously, but he didn't speak.

"Richard," Cecily said, her voice surprisingly smooth as she once again reached for the carton. "Thanks for your help."

Richard clung to the box and glared at the man, who stood a good head taller than Cecily. "I think I got 'em all, Mrs. Adams," he declared, his eyes never leaving the man. "I'll carry the box to your car. It's really too heavy—"

"No, Richard, that's all right. I can manage."

Sensing Richard's reluctance to relinquish the papers, the man extended his free arm and swiped the carton from the youth. "I'll carry them to Mrs. Adams's car," he declared.

Richard's frown deepened, and Cecily resolved to take this masquerade to its limit. The idea, after all, was to discourage Richard from continuing to fawn on his teacher. "Richard," she said sweetly. "It's all right. This is my good friend—"

"Nick Faro," the man interceded, removing his arm from Cecily in order to shake Richard's hand. "And who's this young man, *darling*?"

Cecily tried not to wince. What must Nick Faro think of her? Some sort of madwoman, no doubt. But she'd gone this far, so she might as well follow through on it. "This is Richard Pettibone, one of my students."

"Ah, Richard Pettibone." The stranger nodded and cupped his fingers possessively over Cecily's shoulder. "The boy you've told me so much about?"

"Uh—yes," Cecily murmured vaguely, feeling progressively more awkward as the charade continued.

Nick Faro eyed her mischievously. "Well, *love*, it's a pleasure to finally meet Richard after all this time." His voice was soft and alluringly husky. Cecily nervously pursed her lips and attempted to inch a step away from him. He drew her firmly back to his side and his grin expanded. "I mean, just this morning over breakfast, *dear*, weren't you talking about him?''

Cecily suppressed a grimace. "Uh—Nick," she stammered, trying to ward him off with a nearly imperceptible shake of her head. She had a reputation to protect with her students, for heaven's sake! She couldn't have this handsome stranger talking publicly about eating breakfast with her. "No," she said, anxiously trying to repair the damage. "No, when we *met at the restaurant for breakfast* this morning, I told you about another student of mine. You must be mistaken.''

The man's grip tightened, and his dark eyes twinkled with more mischief. "I must be confused, *honey*. Maybe it was yesterday at breakfast when you mentioned Richard to me. Or was it Saturday night, perhaps? Remember, around two o'clock in the morning, after we—''

"No," she said swiftly and sternly. "Please, Nick—" Too flustered to finish her sentence, she pivoted to Richard and said, "You may as well head for home now. I'm sure I have all the papers here.''

"Okay," the boy said hesitantly. He backed up a step, scuffing his sneaker's toe into the patchy grass at his feet. After shooting her a baleful look, he turned and jogged slowly across the asphalt to the street.

"Keep up the good work, Richard!" Nick Faro hollered after him.

Cecily waited until Richard was out of sight before confronting the man. Unnerved by his dark, pulsing gaze, she moistened her lips with her tongue before speaking. "Look...I'm sorry I threw you a curve like that—''

"I'm not sorry at all," he cut her off, smiling enigmatically.

She took a deep breath, inhaling the subtle leather aroma of his jacket. Nick Faro was a startlingly good-looking man.

Before she could let herself respond to his attractiveness, however, she hastily remembered that he'd extended her little game far beyond the bounds of good taste. Her cheeks colored slightly as she recalled his insinuations about breakfasting with her, and about their conversation at two in the morning after they'd...well, whatever. Drawing in another breath, she said, "I only wanted to convince my student that I'm not a suitable object for his infatuation. I'm sorry if I took you by surprise, but you really didn't have to—"

"It was one of the loveliest surprises of my life," Nick murmured. Absorbing her concerned expression, he gave a soft, smoky laugh. "Did I humiliate you?"

"A little," she admitted.

His laughter stopped, but his enchanting smile lingered, "I'm sure most high school kids these days know the score," he said in his defense. "By the time you called me 'sweetheart,' he'd already put two and two together."

"I wouldn't bet on it," Cecily muttered. "He's pretty dense." Her cheeks still glowing, she took the carton from Nick. "Anyway, thanks for helping out," she said, eager to depart before he could humiliate her further.

He took the carton back from her easily and headed toward the lot. "The kid was right about one thing—this box is heavy. Where's your car?"

Whoever said chivalry was dead? Cecily wondered irritably as she led Nick to her sky-blue Volkswagen Rabbit and unlocked the door. Were all the world's men in collusion to keep her from carrying a stupid cardboard box of student themes? Nick set the box on the driver's seat, and her irritation turned to dismay as she noticed the confused jumble of papers. She picked through the top few sheets. "Damn!" she groaned. "Why these kids can't staple their essays together is beyond me."

"Is that what they are? Student essays?"

She nodded grimly. "I tell the kids to staple them and make sure they've got their names somewhere on each page, just in case something like this happens. Damn," she muttered. "I'm going to be spending the better part of the weekend just sorting out this mess."

Sighing, she moved the box onto the passenger seat and then straightened up. Nick was staring at the athletic field beyond the fence, where the football team was executing a drill. Once the play ended, he turned back to Cecily.

"I didn't mean to interrupt you," she apologized. "Go back and watch. I'm all set now, thanks."

Nick shrugged, draping one arm over the car door. "No problem," he assured her. His lips slid into a mischievous smile again. "I hope you're prepared for this evening when you have to explain to your husband why you were calling me 'sweetheart' at the top of your lungs this afternoon."

"My husband?"

Nick's smile faded. "Didn't that boy call you Mrs. Adams?"

"I'm widowed," Cecily explained.

"Ah." He scrutinized her, his eyes registering neither sadness nor pity. Mild surprise, perhaps, curiosity. "In that case, we haven't caused the scandal of the century, have we?"

"You sound almost disappointed, Mr. Faro," Cecily teased.

His eyes glimmered. Definitely curiosity, Cecily assessed his expression. "Glenville could use a little spicing up," he claimed, smiling again. The players on the field broke their formation to take a brief rest, and Nick touched Cecily's arm. "I've got to talk to someone," he said. "Don't go away."

She watched him stroll to the fence. A brawny young man in a practice jersey neared the fence from the other side, tugging off his helmet. Cecily recognized him as Bruce Munsey, one of her senior students, and she drifted closer to listen in on his conversation with Nick.

"Where were you last night?" he asked Bruce.

"Oh, man." Bruce groaned, and raked his fingers through his sand-colored hair. "Coach Doherty called an extra practice yesterday, and then I had to do this essay. For her," he added, pointing to Cecily.

Nick glimpsed Cecily over his shoulder, then turned back to Bruce. "You're telling me it's her fault you didn't show up for work last night?" he asked, waving Cecily over. "Mrs. Adams, Bruce here says that he had to do an essay for you last night, so he couldn't come to work. Is that right?"

Cecily didn't want to interfere in what was obviously none of her business, but Nick was waiting for her to say something. She gave Bruce a dry smile. "You didn't have to do the essay last night, Bruce," she said. "I assigned that paper a week ago. You didn't have to wait till the last minute to write it."

Nick nodded triumphantly. "See? It's not her fault. And it's not the coach's fault either, because you've got a big game tomorrow and he always calls extra practices before a big game. So I guess that makes it your fault, pal."

Bruce scowled. "Aw, come on. Jack Donovan said he'd cover for me."

"Bruce, I'm backed up all over," Nick complained. "If Jack Donovan could do your job in addition to his, do you think I'd have hired you?"

"Hey, what's more important?" Bruce argued. "My schoolwork or being a packing clerk?"

"That's your decision to make," Nick said solemnly. "Think it over, Bruce. Make up your mind and take some responsibility. Don't be such a baby, huh?"

The coach blew his whistle, and Bruce shrugged contritely. "I gotta go, Uncle Nick. I'm sorry about yesterday—it won't happen again." He spun around and ran across the field to join his teammates in another drill.

"Your nephew?" Cecily asked Nick.

He nodded. "Your student?"

"That's right."

"How's he doing?"

She started back to her car, Nick accompanying her. "So-so," she replied. "He's a bright kid. Maybe a bit overextended," she mused. "High-school senior, football star and holding down a job. It's no wonder he's not doing as well as he ought to be."

"You heard what I told him," Nick commented. "He's got to make some decisions. It's up to him."

"Well, if I had to make his decision for him, I'd tell him to quit his job," Cecily remarked bluntly. Even if it was none of her business, she was a teacher and she couldn't help worrying about her students.

She and Nick had reached her car. Nick leaned casually against the hood and folded his arms over his chest. "You think he should quit his job, huh? It's a damned good job. A lot of kids would give their eyeteeth for it."

"A lot of kids haven't got the opportunity your nephew has," Cecily pointed out.

Nick's left eyebrow arched upward. "What opportunity is that?" he asked.

"The school scuttlebut is that he's being courted by a few colleges, that he's got a good shot at winning a football scholarship."

Nick waited, and when Cecily didn't continue, he prodded her. "So?"

"So?" Her eyes widened with amazement. Didn't Nick know what a football scholarship could mean to a boy like Bruce? Not necessarily the chance to play professional football—having been married to a football coach, Cecily knew how bad the odds were against a boy's succeeding in professional sports. But she also knew that Glenville was a dying city, and the youngsters who weren't lucky enough to go to college could look forward to little in the way of a future in their home town. Like so many other mid-sized smokestack towns along the Ohio River, Glenville had seen its industrial base shrink over the past decade. The city's major employer, Glenville Industries, frequently was forced to have lay-offs and temporary shutdowns. The only hope for Glenville's young people, as far as Cecily could tell, was to go to college, learn new skills and do whatever they had to do to avoid following in the footsteps of their underemployed parents.

Bruce Munsey, like most of his schoolmates, didn't have the money to go to college. Nor did he have the outstanding grades he'd need to win an academic scholarship. But he did have his athletic skill. If his exceptional ability to catch a ball was enough to pay his way through a higher education, Cecily was all in favor of it.

She was puzzled by Nick's lack of enthusiasm for his nephew's prospects. So what if Bruce missed his shift as a packing clerk? He'd be better off missing more shifts, she thought. Without an afterschool job, Bruce could keep his grades up and continue his sterling performances on the football field. He could get a scholarship, an education, a real chance in life. Certainly the few dollars an hour he might earn working for his uncle couldn't be as important as that.

She wanted to sound off to Nick, but his dazzling smile caused her words to stick in her throat. His teeth cut a stark white crescent against his bronze complexion. There was something almost cocky about Nick Faro, an arrogance in his posture as he lounged against her car, an unnerving self-confidence in the steadiness of his eyes as they coursed over her. Her lips flexed, but she remained silent.

"So," he murmured, evidently tiring of waiting for her to complete her thought. "Are you free tonight, Mrs. Adams?"

His question was totally unexpected. "I beg your pardon?"

He chuckled. "Maybe I ought to back up a step. What's your first name?"

"Cecily," she told him.

"Cecily," he echoed. "Are you free tonight, Cecily?"

"I..." She felt the corners of her mouth twitching upward. Having moved to Glenville only two months ago, she hadn't dated anyone in town, and she didn't really mind her solitude. On the other hand, she certainly wasn't averse to reactivating her social life. "What did you have in mind?" she asked.

His smile matched hers. "Oh, all sorts of things, *darling*," he teased.

"Maybe you ought to back up a dozen steps," she warned him, though her eyes were sparkling. "You don't want to take advantage of a newcomer, do you?"

"There's nothing I'd rather do than take advantage of you," he murmured roguishly. "But I won't. I'll just take you out to dinner and make you feel a little less like a newcomer. How does that sound?"

"I think I'd like that," she accepted.

"Don't *think* you'd like it," Nick protested. "Just say, 'Yes, *sweetheart,* I'd like that.'"

She laughed. "Yes...*sweetheart*."

"I mean, we don't want that poor kid thinking we were just playing a trick on him, do we, *honey*?"

Still laughing, she shook her head. "Something tells me I never should have done what I did to you today."

"Something tells me you're never going to regret doing what you did to me today," he returned, his tone conveying an implicit challenge. He rose from the fender and ushered Cecily to her door. "Where do you live?"

"Glenville Heights," she told him. "It's an apartment complex up Congdon Street—"

"I know the place," Nick told her, his smile vanishing and his voice oddly harsh. "Up on the hill. Which building are you in?"

She tried to fathom his abrupt coolness at the mention of her address, then shook off her uneasiness. There was nothing at all wrong with where she lived. She needn't be so sensitive about Nick's unexplained reaction. He hadn't withdrawn his invitation, had he? "The second building on the left after you turn onto the entrance driveway. I'm in apartment two-oh-three."

"Good enough," he said, his warm grin taking shape again. "I'll pick you up at six o'clock."

She settled herself on the bucket seat. He shut the door for her, then started back to the athletic field. Rolling down her window, she called out, "Nick? What should I wear?"

He halted and turned back to her. His penetrating eyes roamed from the shimmering reddish-brown waves of her hair to her clear, delicate features, and then downward until the car's door blocked his view of her. He presented her with another heart-melting smile. "Something sexy," he answered before ambling to the athletic field.

Two

Something sexy...

Cecily gave a low laugh as she steered her car up Congdon Street's steep incline to the Heights, Glenville's relatively affluent neighborhood on a cliff overlooking the city. While no part of the weary mill town was truly affluent in the way that the Long Island community where Cecily used to live and teach was, the Heights rose far enough above the gritty downtown area that its sidewalks and trees were never dusted with the soot and grime pouring out of the smoke stacks of the factories along the river. Most of the town's professionals, and the managers and bosses of Glenville Industries and a few smaller plants, lived in large houses along elm-lined boulevards on the cliff. Only a few apartment clusters were located in the area.

Glenville Heights Apartments might have been elegant when they were first built over twenty years ago, but like so much else in Glenville, the complex of two-story apartment buildings was showing its age. The stucco facades of the buildings had faded to a dull grayish hue, and the once-luxurious lobbies now looked drab. But Cecily had chosen to rent a modest one-bedroom apartment in the complex, because the apartments she'd looked at downtown were even grimmer—dark floor-throughs above shops and alleys. The carpeting of her apartment was a short-napped green, which clashed with her flowered blue chintz sectional sofa, but the terrace off the living room offered a breathtaking vista of Glenville, the Ohio River, and the rolling hills beyond. And the rent, at least by Long Island standards, was low.

She wondered if she had only imagined Nick's subtly dis-approving reaction to her address. His eyes had darkened momentarily, his smile had disappeared, his voice had sounded gruff when he'd claimed he knew the place. She couldn't guess why he'd view the Heights less than favor-ably. He might very well live in that part of town himself.

After all, he was probably some sort of business owner or manager. Since he was in a position to hire his nephew as a packing clerk—to say nothing of being able to take off from work in the middle of the afternoon to watch the high-school football team's practice—he must have a position of power at his place of business. Yet his clothes hadn't ex-actly seemed managerial. A pair of jeans and a weathered leather jacket weren't the kind of clothing the president of Glenville Industries would wear.

Well, she thought as she dropped her carton of student papers onto the kitchen table and strolled down the short hallway to her bedroom, she would have plenty of time to learn more about Nick Faro over dinner tonight. After kicking off her shoes, she slid open her closet door and sur-veyed its contents in search of something appropriate to wear for her dinner date. *Something sexy,* she mused. That could mean anything from a chic slacks outfit to a classy dress.

Something sexy. Another laugh escaped her as she undressed and hung up her school clothes. She crossed to the bathroom and turned on the shower, then stepped beneath it. She might not know much about Nick, but his parting comment was enough to persuade her that she'd enjoy spending the evening with him.

It wasn't that she was looking for romance. Far from it. But for the first time since Phil had passed away more than a year ago, a man had approached her not as a widow but as...a woman.

She had only two dates since Phil's death. One was with an old friend of hers and Phil's, and the other was with a fellow who'd been a boyfriend of hers in graduate school, and who'd wound up living not far from her when they both took teaching jobs on Long Island. She hadn't expected Phil's friend to be anything but a gentleman, but Dave...in graduate school, she'd nicknamed him "the octopus" because of his clinging hands during the numerous wrestling matches she'd been through with him. Not that she'd have cared to fight him off again after all those years, but...but for heaven's sake, he needn't have treated her like a nun, a eunuch, a woman whose sexuality had been nailed into the coffin with her husband.

Sometimes she felt guilty about her desire to resume a normal life after Phil's death. In the first months after that devastating evening when a policeman had appeared on her front step and said, "Mrs. Adams, I'm afraid I have some bad news," Cecily had been almost catatonic, hardly able to function. She'd numbly let her parents take care of her, handle things, coddle and protect her. The school had also been compassionate, urging her to take off the rest of the year and pull herself together.

By the end of the Christmas holiday, however, she'd been itching to return to work. She'd grown restless, tired of feeling helpless and unable to control her own life. She'd known that she wouldn't be able to overcome her grief unless she was back in her regular patterns, feeling useful and competent, connecting with her friends and students.

Her parents had been horrified by her decision to resume her usual routine so soon after Phil's death. Their attitude only added to her feelings of guilt. Was there something wrong with a woman who stopped wearing black only a few months after being widowed, who moved back into the house she'd shared with her husband and began to socialize again, to cook her own meals, earn her own salary and live like a human being? Was there something wrong with a woman whose yearning to be loved hadn't disappeared simply because the man she loved had?

No, she assured herself as she lathered shampoo into her hair. No, she mustn't feel guilty. She'd quit her job on Long Island, sold the house and moved to Ohio to get away from the people who, with the best of intentions, seemed determined to make her feel guilty for wanting to become whole again. If she'd learned anything in her marriage, it was that she was a mature, independent woman who had every right to acknowledge and fulfill her own needs.

It was Phil himself who'd made her recognize the woman she was. They'd had their arguments and disagreements, just like any typical married couple, but they'd also had a liberating love, a trust, a respect for each other that transcended the squabbles. Their sex life had been wonderful. Although Cecily had been rather inexperienced when she'd met Phil, he had taught her the beauty of her own body, the joy she was capable of giving and receiving. He never made her feel embarrassed or guilty.

They'd made a pact at the start of their relationship that, no matter what their days had contained in the way of difficulty, they'd never bring their problems to bed with them. Their love life was too special, too precious to be tainted by the quirks and quibbles of daily living. Phil had awakened Cecily to the miracles of love; she frequently used to kid him about taking his profession as a physical education teacher too seriously.

Although they'd been together only six years, Cecily had known Phil better than anyone else had. She knew that he would applaud her efforts to break out of the protective cocoon in which her parents had tried to imprison her. She knew that he'd congratulate her for forging her own way, taking responsibility for herself, venturing out into the world and celebrating life even in his absence. In fact, she was certain that he'd be quite pleased by her decision to have dinner with Nick Faro, a man who'd recommended that she wear something sexy. "You're a woman," she heard Phil's voice whisper through the spray of shower water beating down on her head. "You're a woman, Cecily, even without me. So for heaven's sake, *be* a woman!"

She shut off the faucets and wrapped her damp body in an oversized towel. Stepping out of the tub, she studied her reflection in the mist-shrouded mirror above the sink. Her cheeks were flushed, her green eyes glowing, her mouth curving into a shy smile. No matter how sexy an outfit she wore tonight, she couldn't imagine ever sleeping with Nick—in all honesty, she couldn't imagine sleeping with any man but Phil. Yet the way Nick had approached her earlier in the afternoon delighted her. For Phil's sake—for her *own* sake—she would be a woman tonight.

Once she had blow-dried her hair, she returned to her bedroom and selected a slim-fitting sheath of a tawny knit fabric that highlighted her coloring. With its simple lines and high neck, it wasn't sexy in an obvious way. But it out-lined her lithe figure, flattering her tiny waist and the well-proportioned curves of her breasts and hips; and the small slit rising from the hem on one side offered a glimpse of sleek legs. Phil had adored the way the dress looked on her. She hadn't worn it since he died, but now it seemed like the right time to take it out of storage.

She brushed her hair and fluffed it out from her shoul-ders, then returned to the bathroom to put on some light make-up and cologne. Back in her bedroom, she added high-heeled brown sandals and a string of pearls to the en-semble, then headed to the kitchen to sort through her stu-dents' papers while she waited for Nick.

He rang for her promptly at six, and the chiming of her doorbell caused her pulse to accelerate slightly. She had no good reason to be nervous about her impending date, yet she couldn't smother the twinge of anxiety that ran up her spine. She was sure that Nick's sly remark about wanting to take advantage of her was just so much teasing. But her shower sermon about how she had a right to date men and to be treated like a woman didn't negate her innate understand-ing that Nick Faro was somehow more than just a man, just a date. He was incredibly sexy, and more than a little for-ward. Maybe, just maybe, she'd bitten off more than she could chew.

She ought to have worn something less suggestive, she chastised herself as she hastened to the door. She ought to have worn that baggy cotton shift with the puffy sleeves that Phil always referred to as her "sweet-sixteen" dress. She ought to have skipped the cologne....

Swallowing, she shored up her courage and endeavored to ignore the panic and doubt that rippled through her. She was a woman, an adult, and she had every right in the world to spend an evening with a man like Nick Faro.

She swung open the door and immediately felt herself being drawn in by his deep-set brown eyes. He wore a well-tailored suit of dark gray wool, and given his neatly groomed appearance she was relieved that she'd chosen to wear a dress rather than slacks. Even in her high-heeled sandals she felt as if he was looming above her. He was taller than Phil, and slightly thinner, built not like a football player but like a basketball player. There was definitely an athletic aspect to his physique.

"You took me at my word," he murmured with pleasure as his gaze traveled down her body. "That's a very sexy dress."

Another twinge of apprehension pulsed through her, but she refused to succumb to it. "I was planning to wear my overalls," she parried, "but they were in the laundry, so I had to make do with this."

"Promise me you'll never do your laundry," he requested, his lips arching into a devilish grin. "Are you all ready?"

"Let me just get my purse," she said, leading him into the living room and then going to her bedroom to fetch her bag. When she returned to the living room she discovered it empty. She spotted Nick outside on the terrace and crossed the room to join him.

"Nice view," he observed, though his smile was gone.

She recalled his chilliness when she'd told him where she lived. In spite of his enjoyment of the panorama stretched out below them, he seemed cool and distant again. "The view was what sold me on the place," she told him. "It isn't the greatest apartment in the world, but the terrace alone is worth the rent."

Curling his fingers about the iron railing, he leaned forward and studied the vista for a silent minute. Then he turned and ushered her through the sliding glass door into the apartment. "It's okay," he commented impassively.

"You don't like it," she guessed. At his quizzical glance, she shrugged "I admit the carpet looks lousy, and my furniture doesn't really fit too well into a room this size, but—"

"Don't apologize," he cut her off, taking her elbow and leading her to the front door.

He said nothing as she locked up the apartment, and his continuing silence as they strolled down the hall to the stairway and descended to the ground floor perplexed her. At the foot of the stairs she halted. "What, Nick?" she demanded. "What's wrong with where I live?"

"Nothing," he answered.

She wasn't convinced. "When I gave you my address this afternoon, you iced up. And now again. Come on, be honest. Did you see a cockroach? Did you use to date someone else who lived here? What?"

Her lack of reserve surprised him, and he studied her speculatively for a moment before chuckling. "No cockroaches, Cecily. No former girl friends." He reflected for a moment. "It's just the Heights in general," he explained with a vague shrug.

"What about the Heights in general?" she prodded him as he held the building's door open for her.

"I grew up in Glenville," he related, his voice even and controlled. "In a town like this, there're two classes of people—people and snobs. The snobs live in the Heights."

"I'm not a snob," she protested.

"Maybe you aren't," he allowed. "It's just a reflex with me, I guess. Some of my best friends live in the Heights and all that. But I'm a Glenville kid from town, blue-collar, dirt-under-my-nails, house-in-the-shadow-of-the-smoke-stack.

The folks in the Heights always looked down on us—literally. Some things you don't forget."

Cecily cast him an appraising look. The collar of his button-down shirt was white, and his fingernails were clean and short. The car he led her to in the front lot of the building was a fire-engine red Porsche. Not exactly the make of automobile one would expect of a poor boy from the wrong side of town.

She said nothing as he helped her onto the low-slung seat and then climbed in behind the wheel. "Maybe you come from humble beginnings," she observed tartly, "but judging by this vehicle, you seem to have made your way to the top."

"The top of what?" he posed, not at all offended by her mildly critical tone. "Not the top of Glenville. I still live downtown." Coasting down the driveway to the avenue, he laughed. "Do you always shoot from the hip, Cecily, or do I bring out the bluntness in you?"

She matched his laughter. "I'm usually pretty blunt," she told him.

"Good." He steered north on the avenue, away from the downtown area to the outskirts of Glenville. "When you told me where you lived I thought you might be a snob, so I made a reservation at the snobbiest joint in town. I hope you don't mind."

"The snobbiest joint in town, huh," she said, joking. "I hope I remember which fork to use."

The restaurant he drove to was housed in a sprawling Victorian manor not far from the farmlands which spread north of the town. The first floor of the house had been refurbished as a huge dining room, its decor unassuming but pleasant. In the far corner of the room was a small dance floor; a three-piece combo performed mellow background music. Nick gave his name to the hostess, who led them to a small table near a window overlooking a garden, and lit the centerpiece candle for them.

Cecily scanned the room before taking her seat. "This is lovely, Nick," she acknowledged. It didn't seem particularly snobbish to her. That Nick thought it was indicated something about him, but she wasn't sure what. "Do you really think I'm a snob?" she asked, as he settled in his seat across from her.

He grinned and raked a shock of black hair back from his brow with his hand. "I don't know what you are, Cecily," he commented softly. "Except that you're a woman."

"I'm a teacher," she reminded him pointedly, wondering once again whether she was ready to handle a man as forward as Nick.

His smile broadened. "How would you rather be thought of, as a teacher or a woman?" he challenged her.

"I didn't know they were mutually exclusive," she shot back.

He laughed and turned to the waitress who had approached their table to take their drink orders. Cecily requested a scotch and soda, Nick a bourbon straight up.

He turned his attention back fully to Cecily. His eyes seemed fathomless to her, resoundingly dark. She detected laugh lines framing their outer corners and found herself wondering how old he was. At least he wasn't a high-school junior like Richard Pettibone, the only male in Glenville who'd taken an interest in her until that afternoon.

"So tell me, blunt schoolteacher woman," he gently teased her. "What do you think of Glenville?"

"It's...interesting," she said tactfully. "Not exactly what I'm used to."

"What are you used to?"

She waited for the waitress who was delivering their drinks to leave before she replied. "I'm from Long Island, outside

New York City. Except for the four years I was away at college, I spent my entire life there. My teaching job there was in a town about twenty miles from where I grew up."

"What brought you here?" he asked.

She paused before answering. Studying him as he relaxed in his chair, she admired the vivid contrast of his long tan fingers against the white linen table cloth. She relished the husky rumble of his voice, the intense glow of his eyes as he awaited her answer. Even if she weren't by nature a blunt person, Nick Faro was the sort of man who demanded honesty. "My husband died over a year ago," she replied, silently praying that he wouldn't pity her. "He'd taught at the same school I taught at, and while I wound up finishing my contract there, I just didn't feel like staying on. So I sent out some inquiries, and Glenville High School had an opening for someone with my background. So here I am."

He leaned back slightly, measuring her with his gaze. "Any regrets?"

Yes, of course she had regrets, she almost answered. She regretted that Phil had to die, that he had to be driving on the same road at the same time as a crazed drunkard. She regretted that the last time she'd seen him alive they'd quarreled. He'd shown up at her classroom as she was preparing to leave and told her he was planning to hold a late practice that afternoon. She'd angrily reminded him that he'd promised to spend the evening with her at one of the local shopping malls, browsing for an anniversary present for her parents. He in turn had sworn that he'd told her he might have to hold an extended practice with his team. What a silly, trivial thing to argue about.

But they'd argued, and she'd stormed from the school, fuming about his forgetfulness, pondering whether he'd deliberately put her parents' impending anniversary party out of his mind because he wasn't exactly in love with his in-laws. She'd driven home, changed her clothing, and shut herself in the den with a stack of student papers to grade. Muttering and slashing at the students' essays with her red pen, she'd listened for the sound of Phil's key in the front-door lock. Instead she'd heard the doorbell, and when she'd answered it she'd found a police officer standing on the front step, his hat in his hand and his face downcast. "I'm sorry, Mrs. Adams. I'm afraid I have some bad news...."

It occurred to her that Nick was waiting for her to speak, and she groped for her drink and took a long sip to clear her mind. When she lifted her eyes, she found him angling his head, trying to read her. "Regrets?" she mumbled. "About coming to Glenville, you mean? No, not yet."

He weighed her comment. Cecily suspected that he was trying to decide whether or not to question her about the strange silence she'd temporarily lapsed into. He chose instead to say, "Not yet? Planning to have regrets in the future?"

His good-natured smile and his gentle humor appealed to her, and she relaxed in her chair. "I'm not very good at reading the future, Nick," she remarked. "If I was..."

"If you were...?"

"Maybe my husband would still be alive today," she concluded. "Maybe I would have known that he shouldn't be driving home that evening, or that he should have taken a different route."

"He was in a car accident?" Nick guessed. At Cecily's nod, he scowled. "Jesus. What a waste."

His comment startled her. Not "Oh, such a terrible shame," not "You poor, poor thing," but "What a waste." Her sentiments exactly. Phil's death had been a waste, a cheap trick of fate, a meaningless loss. Once she had overcome her initial grief, she'd come to view the accident exactly as Nick had described it: a waste.

Nick was, she realized, a refreshing change from all the teary, supersensitive people she usually met. He didn't seem to feel sorry for her; indeed, he didn't seem to believe there was anything about her that he should feel sorry for. There wasn't, she reminded herself. She was living her life, coping well, deriving pleasure and fulfillment from her work. Surely she was better off than many people. She had her intelligence, her education, her career. She was teaching at a school where she could make a difference, where students could profit from what she had to offer. She was attractive, and she was healthy.

And she was in the company of a man who didn't want to drown her in cloying pity. She smiled at Nick and nodded. "Yes," she agreed. "It was a waste, but...These things happen, I guess, and there isn't a whole lot anyone can do about them."

He smiled as well, then accepted the menus the waitress brought them. They spent several minutes discussing the dinner choices before deciding on prime ribs.

"How about you?" she inquired, once the waitress had taken their orders and left. "A native Glenviller, I take it. Have you ever lived anywhere else?"

"Other than an extended all-expense-paid vacation in Southeast Asia, I've always lived here," he replied, giving his bourbon a brief inspection before drinking some. "I love this town."

"Do you really?" While Cecily was glad for the change of scenery Glenville offered her, and even gladder to be far from her doting parents, she didn't think Glenville was particularly lovable. "It's a decaying old city with a dying industrial base," she pointed out. "How can you love it?"

He sat up straighter, his eyes glinting at her insult to his home town. "Who says it's dying?" he argued. "Some companies may be having their problems, but other companies are moving in to fill the gap. Glenville's going through some difficulties, sure, but it isn't dead yet.''

Cecily chuckled. "Don't tell me you're one of those bombastic civic boosters."

Nick remained solemn. "If I can make a go of it here, anyone can," he insisted. "People like to throw up their hands and surrender, but not me. I was born in this town, I learned about life in this town, and now I'm giving something back to this town. Glenville and I get along pretty well these days."

"What are you giving back?" she asked.

Their salads arrived, but Nick ignored his. "I started a business here, and it's doing well, well enough to hire a lot of people and fork out a lot of taxes."

"And pay its founder enough money to buy a bright red Porsche," Cecily added with an impish grin. "If that's not a snobbish car, I don't know what is."

His soft, easy laughter filled the air between them. "Okay, so I drive a fancy car," he confessed. "One small status symbol. I guess I'm entitled to that."

"What sort of business do you have?" she asked.

"O.R. Enterprises. Industrial trouble-shooting." At her curious smile, he continued. "Some company has a problem that they can't figure out how to solve. My people go in and solve it."

"Just like that?"

He laughed again. "We don't exactly wave magic wands, but we bring in fresh ideas and try to show the company some solutions it's overlooked or ignored." He picked at his salad as he explained. "Before I left for 'Nam, I worked for Glenville Industries. I used to work a piece of machinery that jammed up whenever it got too hot. The company's solution was to keep the room air-conditioned year-round. They were spending a fortune on air-conditioning, plus making the men who worked in that room damned uncomfortable." He set down his fork and reminisced. "While I was away...well, there were a few things you could do to survive in 'Nam. You could do drugs, go nuts, get mad. I used to think instead. I'd think about my former job, about that ridiculous air-conditioning and the machine always threatening to jam up, and I figured that if there was a way to enclose the machine in some sort of refrigerated jacket, you wouldn't have to freeze the whole room."

He paused to drink some bourbon. "And?" Cecily prompted him.

"And then I got home, and Glenville Industries told me they didn't have a job for me anymore," he went on, his tone momentarily touched with bitterness. "So I said, 'Keep the job but hear me out. I think I can solve this jamming problem for you.' I sketched a few pictures for them, and they were interested enough to tell me to do some estimates and figure out how much the shield would cost."

"Do you have an engineering background?" Cecily asked.

He shook his head. "No, but this buddy of mine in 'Nam did. Snooty kid from M.I.T. I phoned him up, laid it out for him, and he came to Glenville to help me on it. Next thing I knew, we were starting up O.R."

"Why O.R.? Are those his initials?"

He laughed. "It stands for 'Orphan Running.'"

"Orphan Running?" Cecily echoed in bewilderment. "Are you an orphan?"

Nick shook his head again. "Orphan, like—ever hear of orphan drugs? Those are drugs that can be used to treat rare diseases. None of the big drug companies like to manufacture them, because maybe three people have the disease and the company can't make a profit producing on such a small scale. What we do is kind of like that, solving rare problems, but industries are usually willing to pay for a solution if it's going to save them money in the long run." He lowered his glass. "Anyway, my partner was always saying, 'Pull this project together and we'll be off and running.' It's kind of an inside joke."

"I take it it's quite a successful inside joke," Cecily mused, fascinated by Nick's tale. He seemed the very embodiment of an American success story, living proof of the message she was trying to convey to her students: be smart; use your brains; make something of yourselves. Don't limit yourselves to Glenville Industries. Get an education and try something new.

The waitress delivered their dinners. Nick nodded his approval. "Jim—my partner—was the one to recommend this place. I guess we won't have to fight about it the next time I see him."

"Do you and he fight often?"

"Constantly," Nick admitted with a smile. "We're water and oil, Jim and me. *He* lives in the Heights."

"But you work well together.?"

"Thank God for that," Nick confirmed. "The guy's brilliant. Snobby s.o.b., but absolutely brilliant. I come up with the ideas, and he works out their feasibility. I'd be up the creek without him."

Cecily ate her dinner while her mind digested what Nick had told her about himself. Like her he was blunt, and she appreciated his candor. The success of his company was definitely something he deserved to be proud of, yet he seemed equally proud of his proletarian roots, his living "downtown." He wasn't like Phil, or like any other man she'd ever met, but that only increased her fascination.

The trio of musicians began a medley of 'Forties love songs, and Nick set down his silverware and raised his eyebrows. "Should we cut the rug?" he asked.

"Cut the rug?" she blurted out with a laugh.

"Hey, if they're going to play this fuddy-duddy music, I'm going to use the proper lingo," he said, rising from his chair and moving around the table to help Cecily to her feet. They wove among the tables to the dance floor and he gathered her into a discreet embrace. "What's so funny?" he asked as he peered down at her and found her grinning.

Her green eyes twinkled with amusement. "You are," she answered frankly. She recalled the way he'd playfully distorted her ruse that afternoon in the parking lot for Richard Pettibone's benefit, and his clear refusal to express pity for her, and his invitation to cut the rug. "You're a pretty funny guy."

"Is that good or bad?"

"Good," she assured him. "It's very good."

"Hmm." He pulled his arm more snugly around her shoulders, easing her head against his shoulder. "Don't forget, Cecily, you were the one who started the funny business—calling me 'sweetheart' to fake out that student of yours."

She again recalled his enthusiastic participation in her charade, and her chagrin. "Actually, I didn't think it was so funny at the time," she objected, though her voice was muffled by the soft wool of his blazer. She liked the feel of his arms around her, the firm expanse of his shoulder as he led her about the floor. When was the last time a man had held her this way?

"What do you think now?" he murmured, toying with the silky ends of her hair.

She wasn't sure what he was referring to—the afternoon's "funny business" or the sheer pleasure of dancing with him. His grip was strong but understated, and when his thighs brushed lightly against hers she felt a powerful heat infiltrate her, a heady sensation she hadn't known in two long, solitary years. She sighed.

"Still alive down there?" he whispered into her hair.

"Very much alive," she answered throatily.

"You know, you're an exceptionally beautiful woman," he commented. Moving in time to the music, Nick led her from the center of the dance floor to its darkest, most remote corner. It didn't even occur to Cecily to question where he was taking her, or why. She liked the shadowy privacy of the corner, the intimacy of it.

He drew her even closer to himself and touched his lips to her brow. "I don't blame that kid for going bananas over you," he whispered.

"I'm much too old for him," she countered, her voice sounding vague and distant to her.

"You aren't too old for me," he swore, kissing her brow again.

Her breasts pressed into his chest as his arms closed fully around her. She felt her body's instantaneous response to him, to the lean contours of his torso, the easy shifting of his hips against hers. Her mouth instinctively moved to the warm hollow of his throat.

She felt his soft groan as much as heard it. It had the same effect on her as his embrace, as his strong body cradling hers. She felt as if her flesh were being deluged with feeling after a lengthy drought, swamped by the yearning that washed over her. Its immeasurable force shocked her, but she couldn't deny what was happening to her.

She wanted Nick. She wanted to be held, kissed, loved. It had been too long.

She tilted her head back and he covered her mouth with his. His lips played softly over hers, gentle teasing caresses that dazzled her. His hand slid deep into her hair, holding her head steady as the mesmerizing light of his eyes poured over her upturned face.

He kissed her again, and she closed her eyes as another hot wave of sensation swept through her. She felt Nick's tongue testing the seal of her lips and they willingly parted for him. As his tongue filled her mouth her arms tightened around him, relying on him for balance as one wave and then another undermined her equilibrium. She lost consciousness of her surroundings, their secluded corner, the distant music. All she knew was that she wanted to keep kissing Nick, moving with Nick, losing herself to Nick....

Or maybe it wasn't Nick, she thought hazily as she slid her lips from his and tried to regain her bearings. Maybe it wasn't Nick. She hardly knew him; they'd only just met. Maybe she was just hungering for a man—any man—to love her the way Phil had loved her. Maybe she was just a lonesome widow looking for company....

She couldn't. She couldn't do that, either to Nick or to herself. It wasn't right. It wasn't fair. She no longer knew what she wanted, but whatever it was, it was wrong.

She pulled back from him, and he loosened his hold on her. His lids were lowered, his eyes dreamily expressing his own desire as he scrutinized her. "What?" he mouthed.

She eased fully out of his arms and sucked in her breath. "I think we'd better go," she choked out.

"Fine with me," he concurred. Realizing that he'd misinterpreted her statement, she cringed.

Agitated, she hovered beside him at their table while he settled the check. As soon as he'd pocketed his receipt, she darted for the door, anxious to get some fresh air, to get some perspective on what had happened to her during their dance.

Night had fallen, and the clear sky was dotted with glittering silver stars. She hugged her arms to herself and gulped in the cool air, striving for lucidity. Nick slipped his arm around her shoulders. "Chilly?" he asked.

She shook her head. "Nick—I'm sorry—" she stammered. "I think you'd better take me home."

He frowned slightly, bowing his head to study her. "Something bothering you?"

"No. Yes," she floundered.

When she didn't elaborate, he asked, "Did I do something wrong?"

"No," she insisted. "No, Nick—it's me."

"What's you?"

"I—" She swallowed, determined to be as blunt as he expected her to be. "Nick, I wanted you...while we were dancing inside."

He smiled in bemusement. "I noticed," he murmured. "The feeling's mutual, Cecily, so don't feel so bad about it."

"No, I mean..." His smile was so endearing, his puzzlement so evident, that she laughed wistfully. "Nick. It's been so long for me...since my husband died, I mean...I don't know if it was *you* I wanted or just...just a man. God, that sounds horrible," she muttered sheepishly, averting her face. "I'm not the sort of woman who just wants a man. I don't even know *what* I want, Nick, but—"

He touched his fingers to her lips to silence her. "It's okay," he whispered, brushing a stray tear from her cheek. She hadn't even been aware that she was crying. "No problem. I'll take you home."

They drove back to her apartment without speaking. Cecily stared at her hands clenched in her lap and tried to overcome her edginess, her embarrassment, her confusion. She couldn't have truly wanted Nick—she didn't know him well enough to want him. Yet what she did know, she liked.

She liked his personality, his company, his dark eyes, his tender lips...

She shook her head and tried once again to unravel her tangled thoughts. Perhaps it was merely because he was the first man in the past two years to treat her like a woman that she'd responded so overwhelmingly to him. Any man who would treat her like a woman— No, not any man. Nick was unique. She was sure of it. Shooting him a quick glance, seeing his ruggedly chiseled profile as he steered down the avenue to her apartment complex, studying the sharp angle of his jaw, the slight movement of his adam's apple as he swallowed, the tapered length of his fingers curled around the leather-wrapped steering wheel, convinced her that Nick wasn't just any man. When she'd found herself melting in his embrace on the dance floor, she'd been responding not just to a man but to him.

He braked to a stop before her building and twisted in his seat to face her. "You must hate me," she mumbled into her lap, grimacing as she thought of how brazenly she'd encouraged his kisses at the restaurant, and how abruptly she'd broken from him.

"Hate you?" He laughed quietly. "Fat chance."

She met his gaze and sighed. "Then you think I'm off my rocker."

"A little confused, maybe," he granted, running his finger along the smooth arch of her cheekbone. "I won't hold it against you."

"It's just—this is the first real date I've had since my husband died, Nick, and I'm out of practice."

"Your first real date, huh," he mused, letting his hand come to rest on her shoulder. "I'd be happy to give you all the practice you need."

His amused grin elicited a matching smile from her. "Even after I botched things up this time?"

"First time's always rough going," he reassured her. "Why don't we try again tomorrow?"

Her eyes widened with surprise. Either Nick was fool-hardy or he was genuinely interested in her, despite her erratic behavior. Or both. "What about tomorrow?" she asked hesitantly.

"Breakfast."

"Oh no!" She rolled her eyes and groaned. "Then you'll be running through the schoolyard shouting about what we discussed over breakfast and tearing my reputation to shreds."

"That sounds like fun," he teased.

She shared his quiet laugh, then demurred. "Breakfast is out. In case you forgot, I've got a carton full of out-of-order student papers to grade."

"Make it brunch, then," he compromised. "And afterwards we can go to the high school football game. It's my responsibility as an uncle to watch Bruce play. Will you join me?"

"Nick—I really do have to grade papers," Cecily insisted.

"Don't be such a teacher," he chided her. "I like you better when you're a woman." He leaned across the stick shift, kissed her lightly, then climbed out of the car to escort her to the door.

Three

——

Cecily lay awake beneath the blanket for hours, her mind swirling with thoughts of Nick Faro. Had she been responding to *him*, or merely to his overwhelming masculinity? Was she simply a parched wanderer willing to drink from any well, or was it Nick himself who had reawakened her long-dormant sensuality?

She could imagine what Phil would have said about what had occurred between her and Nick: "What's your problem, Cecily? Invite him in—enjoy yourself."

But Phil had always been much looser about sex than Cecily. He'd never tired of taunting her about her reticence with him the first few months they'd dated, about her archaic prudishness. "Don't tell me I've got to marry you in order to get you into bed!" he used to roar with pretended dismay, even though his charge had come terribly close to the truth. She'd debated that men were different from women, that it was inherently easier for men to be casual about sex, and Phil had in turn claimed that most modern women weren't so hung up about it. Cecily was a throwback, he'd complained, an anomaly in the twentieth century. When she'd finally surrendered and let him make love to her, she'd come to think that perhaps he was right. If only she'd known how beautiful love would be with him, she might not have resisted him for so long.

Yet sex with Phil had been beautiful because she loved him, she adored him, she cared for him in a way she'd never before cared for a man. They'd been friends, confidants, lovers in spirit long before they became lovers in the flesh, and Cecily was sure that their emotional bond was what had enabled them to forge such a strong physical bond.

She had no emotional bond with Nick Faro. Liking him wasn't enough, she tried to convince herself. No matter what her body had been telling her at the restaurant, she knew that she'd have been unable to experience with him the ecstasy she'd known with Phil. "Love," she used to argue in her own defense, "is a state of mind. I know that's hard for a physical education teacher to believe, but the only reason you're such a hot-shot in bed is that I happen to love your personality." Phil would invariably make some comment about how in bed his personality was centered somewhere below his waist, and they'd usually dissolve in laughter—and more lovemaking.

It wouldn't be that way with Nick, Cecily admitted. It couldn't be. He wasn't Phil; nothing would ever be the same without Phil. Lying on her wrinkled sheets, her head sinking disconsolately into the down pillows, Cecily found herself missing her husband more than she'd missed him in months.

She arose shortly after dawn and dressed in a pair of brown corduroy jeans, an oxford shirt, and a mustard-colored crew-neck sweater. Nick wouldn't be calling for her

until eleven, so she had several hours to grade papers before he arrived. She fixed herself a strong cup of coffee and
settled at her kitchen table with the carton of essays and a
red pen.

Her students at Glenville High, while bright, weren't as
well prepared for school as her Long Island pupils had been.
Gary Czymanski had often described to her the sorry
standards of the town's grammar schools: overcrowded
classrooms, harried teachers, a lack of creative facilities.
The parents of Cecily's students didn't seem involved
enough in their children's academic careers, either. On Long
Island, whenever one of Cecily's students received a low
grade on an assignment, she received frantic telephone calls
from his parents, questioning her about where the student
was falling behind and what could be done to improve his
performance. Not a single parent had attempted to call her
or meet with her in the month she'd been teaching at Glenville High.

Well, she allowed, her students' parents had problems of
their own. Glenville Industries was threatening another shut-
down; the jet engines the company manufactured weren't in
as much demand as they'd once been, and other nations
could provide the airline industry with engines of equal
quality for less money. The majority of Cecily's students
were the sons and daughters of Glenville Industries employees, and those whose parents worked elsewhere were
similarly afflicted. Whenever Glenville Industries laid its
workers off, the entire town suffered.

Setting aside the several papers she'd graded and shuf-
fling through the stack of essays in search of Bruce Munsey's, Cecily reflected on Nick's chauvinistic pride in
Glenville. Just because he'd succeeded in a failing town
didn't mean that everyone could. Undoubtedly he had certain things going for him that others lacked. He was clever

and knowledgeable. He was willing to take risks. He was obviously quite intelligent. She wondered why he seemed less than enthusiastic about the possibility that his nephew could obtain the sort of education he himself must have benefited from.

Locating Bruce's essay, she shoved back the box and began to read. Bruce's handwriting was wretched, and when she could decipher his scrawling she found it riddled with spelling errors. Even if she hadn't known that he'd procrastinated in writing it until the night before the paper was due, she would have been able to detect its rushed quality. However, his thoughts were sound, and he'd obviously done the required research. He cited the proper sources, and his bibliography, while lacking the correct form, indicated that at least he knew enough to give credit to the authors he'd quoted.

She reread the paper, marking the grammatical mistakes, and jotted a note referring him to the MLA's guidebook on bibliographic style. She was printing a large C-plus at the top of the page when she heard the doorbell sound.

Like the night before, she felt a prickle of apprehension at Nick's arrival. But this morning the reason behind it was different. Last night she'd wondered whether she could handle Nick; this morning she wondered whether she could handle herself. He'd seen her at her worst last night, her snarled emotions fully exposed, and he'd proven his honor and worth by accepting and forgiving her. But now that they were both aware of how vulnerable she was to him, she wasn't sure how he would treat her, or how she'd respond.

Inhaling, she straightened her sweater, shook the legs of her slacks down over her high leather boots, and marched to the door to open it. Clad in jeans, a ribbed dark red turtleneck, and sneakers, Nick appeared wide awake and en-

ergetic. He bowed to kiss her cheek. "Good morning," he
greeted her. "Are you a teacher or a woman today?"

"Both," she replied, unable to suppress her smile at his
jovial mood. "I've just been going over your nephew's paper."

"That's between you and him," Nick declared, apparently uninterested in Bruce's grade—or else simply showing
respect for what was, in fact, a private matter between the
student and the teacher. "No more work for the next few
hours, schoolmarm. We've got to get us some food."

"Yes, sir," she said, touching her hand to her forehead in
a mock salute. She went to the bedroom to get her purse,
then returned to the living room and left the apartment
along with Nick.

The late-morning air was unseasonably warm, the sky
clear and sunny. Nick shoved the sleeves of his sweater up
toward his elbows, revealing his strong, sinewed forearms
and an expensive-looking watch on his left wrist. As he
opened the passenger door of his Porsche for Cecily, she was
once again reminded of the strange blend of successful entrepreneur and city boy he personified. Once he'd joined her
in the car, she asked, "Are we going to another snobby joint
today?"

"Today," he replied as he revved the engine, "we're going
to a *real* joint. Brunch Glenville style. But first, a little
drive."

He steered out of the complex and down the hill towards
the heart of the city. Cecily arranged herself comfortably in
the seat, curious about where Nick was planning to take her.
Her concern about the possibility that things would be
awkward between them after her behavior the previous night
waned as he smiled lazily and whistled an old rock tune.

He turned onto Main Street. "This is downtown Glenville," he announced.

Cecily laughed. "Nick, I know what Main Street looks like," she defended herself. "I live here too, you know."

He cast her a sidelong glance. "You live in the *Heights*," he emphasized. "How often do you come down the hill?"

"Every day," she asserted. "The high school's one block over." But she conceded silently that, other than commuting to and from the school, she rarely visited the downtown district. She did most of her shopping at the supermarket in the Heights.

Main Street was a straight four-lane boulevard lined with small shops and offices. Many of them displayed stickers of the Glenville Tiger, the high school football team's mascot, on their paned glass doors. Upstairs windows in some of the buildings contained signs announcing dentists' and chiropractors' offices, law firms and loan companies, second-hand clothing stores and palm-readers' boudoirs. The buildings tended to be old and seedy, constructed of brownstone, fieldstone, brick, or shingle.

"What do you think?" Nick asked as he waited for a red light in front of the dreary City Hall building.

Cecily shrugged. The town had a homeliness about it, an ugly sort of warmth. She certainly didn't love it, though. "It's kind of charming...I guess," she admitted.

Nick grunted. "Where's that bluntness you're famous for?" he goaded her.

"Okay," she relented. "It's grungy and run-down. Well past its heyday."

Nick grunted again, accepting her honest assessment of his city although he obviously wasn't pleased by it. "What did your town on Long Island look like?" he questioned her.

"Less crowded," she replied. "More greenery. The stores were newer, and they didn't seem to be leaning on each other, the way they do here."

"In other words, no character," he summarized, his grin softening his criticism. He turned the corner and drove down a residential street. Its houses were tall and narrow, separated by paved strips of driveway. The front yards of most were neatly tended, several flashing the golden color of late-blooming marigolds and mums. "That's where I grew up," he said, rolling to a near-stop before a modest brick house with a sagging wooden front porch.

Cecily studied the house intently. Its chimney was rimmed with soot, and paint flaked from the windowsills and the porch railing. It struck her as ramshackle and forlorn, but she didn't dare to say so to Nick. "It must be nice to live within walking distance to town," she noted diplomatically.

"What you're really thinking is, it's a dive," said Nick.

"I didn't say that," she objected.

"But that's what you're thinking."

She turned to face him and his enigmatic half-smile encouraged her to state the truth. "It isn't exactly Buckingham Palace," she commented.

"No," he agreed. "But it's home."

"Is it? I mean, do you still live there?"

He proceeded to the corner and turned right. "My folks do," he told her. "They've got my bedroom all done up upstairs. The furniture dusted, the bed made, everything in place. God knows why," he added with a chuckle. "I haven't got any plans to move back in."

"That's just the way it is with parents sometimes," Cecily said, then sighed. Her parents still had her bedroom in their spacious split-level home waiting for her: fresh linens on the bed, Swiss-dot drapes framing the window, all her stuffed animals lined up like soldiers in the hutch above her French Provincial bureau. After Phil's accident, her parents had insisted that she move in with them until she recovered from her shocking loss, and she'd felt absolutely ridiculous lying in her single bed every night and seeing all those pairs of button-eyes staring down at her from the hutch. "I keep telling my parents to sell my old furniture and turn my room into a guest room or a study, but they won't listen."

"That's the way it is with parents," Nick mimicked with a grin. He cruised along the road, traveling west from his parents' house. Cecily peered down the side streets, spotting several young girls playing hopscotch on one block and a group of boys engaged in a rowdy game of stickball on another. "I live down there," Nick remarked, pointing toward another crowded road of grim narrow houses.

"Isn't your house on the grand tour?" she asked playfully.

He eyed her and laughed. "My house," he answered, "is on the *private* tour. I don't think you're up to that yet."

Cecily turned away and bit her lip. Nick's comment was perceptive, and it disturbed her. She definitely wasn't ready to take a private tour of his house with him, but she wasn't sure she wanted to be kidded about it.

She covered her nervousness by asking, "How old are these houses, anyway?"

"They were built, oh, sixty, seventy years ago," Nick informed her. "Back when Glenville Industries started, they had to provide housing for all the workers they were importing to the area. Most of these houses went up then."

Cecily conjured a mental picture of the relatively new neighborhood she'd been raised in on Long Island. An "old" house in that New York City bedroom community was one that had been standing for more than thirty years. The house she'd lived in had been brand new when her parents had purchased it twenty-three years ago, the lawn newly sodded, the shrubs young and scrawny, the trees mere

saplings. The house she'd shared with Phil had been a fif-
teen-year-old raised ranch on a half-acre of land. She'd
considered it tiny and ancient when they'd bought it. Seeing
Nick's neighborhood revised her perspective.

They drove away from the residential part of town, moving south toward the river. They passed the Shipley Mill, a
fairly small plant where ball bearings were manufactured, and
another factory which had closed down years ago. Beneath a
rusted train trestle, Nick pulled to the side of the road and
braked. "This was my hang-out as a kid," he said.

"Here?" Cecily blurted out, comparing the gloomy, lit-
tered underpass to her own childhood hang-out, a mani-
cured playground five blocks from her house. "You played
beneath the train tracks?"

"Me and my buddies," Nick replied, nodding nostalgi-
cally. His gaze took in the motley graffiti painted over the
concrete supports and he grinned. "Somewhere in that mess
are my initials," he said, heaving himself out of the car and
moving to the cement wall nearest them.

Cecily climbed out and walked over to the wall. "Don't
you think the paint would be worn off by now?"

He scanned the wall, frowning slightly, then smiled and
extended his index finger. "Hey, I wasn't a fool. We didn't
paint our initials—we carved them." He pointed out the
ragged notches in the wall: "N.F.—that's you-know-who,"
he murmured, his finger shifting. "Here's T.C.—Tom Civ-
itelli. And L.S.—Lou Stivitz."

"Your buddies?" Cecily asked. "Are they still in Glenville?"

"Lou and I see each other all the time," said Nick. "I was
his best man a few years back."

"How about Tom?"

Nick's brow darkened and he turned back to the car. "He
didn't make it back from 'Nam," he said.

Cecily fell silent as she joined him in the car. They might both have parents who kept their childhood bedrooms intact like shrines, but the differences between her and Nick were marked. Nobody she'd known when she was growing up had served in Vietnam. Most of the boys had won student deferments, and the few unlucky ones who couldn't avoid service had parents with enough clout to win them tours of duty in Germany or South Korea. She knew the war had been fought largely by poor boys, and sitting beside one such poor boy made her background seem spoiled and pampered by comparison.

Nick's cheerful spirits returned as he guided his sportscar along the ribbon of road bordering the sprawling Glenville Industries property. The parking lots were full of cars. A good sign, Cecily contemplated. If the plant was open for weekend shifts, perhaps lay-offs weren't imminent.

"This is Glenville Industries," Nick unnecessarily told her.

"I know that," she bristled. "Nick, maybe I live in the Heights, but I don't live in a padded cell. I know where Glenville Industries is."

"That's true," he mused, winking. "You can see it from that snobby terrace of yours."

Cecily felt her defenses rising, but she clamped her lips shut and rode out his sly teasing. The only reason she felt so defensive, she acknowledged, was that Nick had pegged her pretty accurately. She wasn't a snob, but she'd lived a privileged life compared to his. His tour through town had just the effect he'd desired; by showing her his childhood home, his hang-out, and the factory that dominated the city's economy, he was telling her more about himself than words could have expressed.

Beyond the fence marking the westernmost edge of Glenville Industries' property stood another plant, its parking lot partially filled with cars. Although the building appeared old, its brick walls were clean and its trim recently painted. Above the entry door hung a sign, white with bright red letters: "O.R. Enterprises." "This is your place!" Cecily identified the plant.

"This is it," Nick confirmed, veering into the driveway and shifting into neutral.

"You run weekend shifts?" she asked.

"Got to. We're kind of backed up these days."

"I suppose that's good news," Cecily observed. "Better to be backed up than waiting for commissions."

Nick smiled and shifted into gear. "One of the reasons Glenville is such a fine place to run a business like this is that there's a fantastic supply of labor. Glenville Industries has shrunk over the years, and when Jim and I got O.R. 'off and running,' we could pick and choose our work force."

"And pay them bargain wages, too," Cecily needled him.

Nick shook his head. "We pay the best wages along the river," he claimed soberly. "Don't forget, Cecily, I did time at Glenville Industries myself. Not that they pay badly, but I know from gut experience that if a worker gets paid a little more he gives back a lot more. I've been there, working ten-hour shifts at mediocre wages in a room as cold as the North Pole. None of that for my people." He drove back to the road leading to town. Once the car was in high gear, he reached across his seat to squeeze Cecily's shoulder. "Now you've seen the sights. I bet you're starving."

"Reasonably hungry," she agreed. "And of course I'm just dying to see what a *real* Glenville brunch is like."

A *real* Glenville brunch, Cecily learned, was an overstuffed three-egg omelet, toasted English muffins and jam, and an endless supply of coffee consumed at a Formica-topped table in a poorly lit diner called Darlene's situated in a back alley at the western edge of the business district. The waitresses all knew Nick by name, and the prices were ridiculously cheap for the vast quantity of food served.

Shoving away her half-eaten omelet, Cecily groaned. "Not another mouthful. I'm absolutely stuffed."

Nick had already polished off all his food, and he helped himself to an untouched muffin-half from her plate. "You can finish that," he chided her, gesturing toward her eggs. "Children are starving in Africa."

"Then let's wrap this up and mail it to them," she suggested, reaching for her coffee. "I don't know about children in Africa, but a woman of my acquaintance in Glenville is going to get very fat if she eats the rest of this omelet."

Nick laughed. "If my mother saw you, she'd click her tongue and say you were nothing but skin and bones."

"But you'd tell her she was wrong," Cecily noted confidently.

"I'd tell her..." His smile grew wistful. "I'd tell her you had the most gorgeous figure I'd ever seen on a woman."

Cecily felt her cheeks coloring, and she took another bracing sip of her coffee. Nick continued to gaze at her, his smile unshakable. She wanted to say something, something about how she still wasn't sure she was ready for things to develop between her and him, but the words didn't come. In a burst of honesty, she admitted that she was thrilled by his compliment. She took enormous pleasure in believing that Nick thought she had a gorgeous figure. How wonderful for a man to treat her like a real woman, without hesitation, without a care about her past troubles.

"Am I humiliating you?" he asked, trying to read her expression.

"Not in the least," she assured him, though her cheeks retained their rosy blush.

"Cecily…" He leaned forward and folded his hand around hers on the table. "About last night—"

"No," she cut him off, suddenly fearful. "Please, let's not talk about it. *That* humiliated me."

"It shouldn't have," he swore. "There's nothing humiliating about wanting a man—even a man like me."

His self-deprecating statement startled her. "Nick, what happened last night had nothing to do with you."

"It had everything to do with me," he argued softly.

"No—I mean…" Slowly it dawned on her why he'd taken her around Glenville, shown her the scenes of his past, given her a tour, not of the town, but of himself and his life. Apparently he thought she'd rejected him last night out of some latent snobbishness. So this norning he'd made a point of letting her know exactly who he was and where he'd come from. "Nick…" She sighed, feeling the piercing darkness of his eyes upon her. "Nick, what happened last night was…" She drifted off uncertainly.

"You wanted me," he supplied for her.

"Yes." She lowered her gaze, afraid for him to see how his directness affected her. "But I don't even know you— last night I knew you less than I know you now. My husband, Nick—I knew him for months and months before I ever felt…"

"Before you ever felt what you felt for me last night?"

"Yes," she whispered.

He lifted her hand to his lips and kissed her palm. "Ah, Cecily," he murmured. "Don't feel humiliated." The corners of his mouth turned upward as he released her wrist and checked his watch. "We've got a game to catch. Alice?" he called to one of the waitresses. "How about the check?"

The parking lot beside the school's football field was already fairly crowded when they arrived. Nick casually took Cecily's hand as they left the car for the rickety wooden bleachers lining the field. He scanned the jammed tiers for a moment, then smiled, waved at someone, and led Cecily to the narrow steps leading up to a central row of seats.

A slim, dark woman lifted her coat from the bench where she'd been holding a place for Nick. He and Cecily excused themselves numerous times as they climbed over already seated football fans to reach the woman. The man beside her, a stocky blond fellow, rose to his feet. "Annie, Al, this is Cecily Adams," he introduced her to the couple. "Cecily, my sister Annie and my brother-in-law Al."

"Hello, Nicholas," Annie said, kissing Nick's cheek in greeting. She offered Cecily a modest smile. "How do you do?"

"Cecily's one of Bruce's teachers," Nick commented as they took their seats, he next to Annie and Cecily on his other side.

Annie leaned across her brother's lap to scrutinize Cecily. "Oh, you're Mrs. Adams? Bruce's social studies teacher?" she asked. At Cecily's friendly nod, her eyes, as dark and piercing as Nick's gave Cecily a probing perusal, and her brows arched upwards. "A teacher, Nicholas?" she whispered, barely loud enough for Cecily to hear.

"Something wrong with that?" he defended himself.

"No," Annie murmured. "It's just...different, that's all."

Cecily shifted uneasily on the narrow bench. When Nick turned to her, she slid towards him and murmured, "What's wrong with my being a teacher?"

Nick presented her with a broad grin. "Annie knows my taste in women doesn't usually run to eggheads," he explained.

"I'm not an egghead!" Cecily protested.

"You know that and I know that," he confided. "Annie hasn't figured it out yet."

Hardly mollified, Cecily frowned and turned towards the field. The marching band played the school's anthem, the musicians' faded uniforms oddly appropriate to their squeaky, out-of-tune performance. Once they took their seats, the opposing team, arch-rivals from a neighboring town, and then Glenville's Tigers raced out onto the field. The crowd erupted in wild cheers.

"Are your parents here?" Cecily asked, laboring to overcome her discomfort at Annie's odd reaction to her.

Nick shook his head. "My father volunteered for a weekend shift today," he told her. "He hates to miss seeing Bruce play, but you can't knock overtime."

The game began. The cheerleaders cheered, the band jangled, the audience responded. Before becoming involved with Phil, Cecily hadn't been a big partisan of scholastic football, but marrying him had entailed becoming the "first lady" of her high school's football team, and she'd learned a great deal not only about the game but about the nature of school sports in general. Phil had been more than just a coach to his boys; he'd been a guidance counselor, a father figure, a friend. Every August before the first practice, she and Phil had hosted a backyard barbecue for his team, and throughout the year the boys frequently dropped by at the house to discuss their problems with him. One of the things she'd loved best about Phil was his treatment of the team, his insistence on benching players when their grades fell, his advice about college and girl friends, his instruction on the importance of good sportsmanship and team trust. She scarcely knew Glenville's football coach, and she watched her new school's team searching for clues about the values he imparted to them.

The Glenville team looked bigger and stronger than the team Phil had coached, but their plays lacked creativity. Bruce Munsey stood out among the otherwise uninspired offensive players, but he alone couldn't carry the team. After a dismal loss on a play, she groaned. "That was a perfect opportunity for a screen play," she muttered in disapproval.

Nick eyed her curiously. "You think so?"

"Either that or a quarterback draw. Coach Doherty ought to update his playbook." The quarterback was sacked, and the Tigers were forced to punt. Cecily shook her head and groaned again.

Nick laughed. "Hey, relax. This isn't the Cincinnati Bengals," he reminded her.

Thanks to a spectacular catch by Bruce on a later offensive series, the Tigers were able to score a touchdown, and at halftime the score was seven-to-nothing in favor of the home team. Although somewhat placated by Glenville's lead, Cecily still couldn't shake the understanding that Coach Doherty wasn't as good a coach as Phil had been.

She and Nick stood to stretch their legs, and she turned to Annie with the vague thought of proving herself to be anything but an egghead. Annie's attention, however, was drawn to a middle-aged, balding man in a suit who was climbing the steps to their bench. She twisted to Nick. "That's Mr. Loden from O.S.U.," she identified the man before waving him over.

A scout from Ohio State University, Cecily surmised with a delighted smile. That Annie knew him indicated that he was here to watch Bruce play.

He edged his way down the bench to them and shook Al's hand. "Hi, Mr. Munsey, Mrs. Munsey," he greeted them. "Fine game Bruce is having."

Annie politely nudged the man towards her brother. "Mr. Loden, this is my brother, Nicholas Faro, and...his friend, Mrs. Adams." Annie's referring to Cecily so formally surprised her until Annie added, "Mrs. Adams is a teacher of Bruce's."

After shaking Nick's hand, Mr. Loden moved closer to Cecily. "One of Bruce's teachers, are you? What subject?"

"Social studies," she replied. "Government systems."

"Government systems?" He weighed that information and grinned. "Is that what we used to call Civics in the olden days?"

"That's right," she confirmed with a grin.

She was acutely aware of Nick's attentive silence, as well as Annie's and Al's, as Mr. Loden cornered her. "Is he a good student?" he asked.

"Good enough for O.S.U., I'm sure," she replied.

He smiled. "That's what I was hoping you'd say," he gushed. "I can't deny I'm impressed with the boy's athletic ability. I'm glad to hear he's got a brain, too."

"Oh, he definitely has a brain," Cecily assured the scout, hoping her enthusiasm about Bruce's potential wasn't too obvious. How wonderful it would be for a boy like Bruce to attend a fine school like Ohio State. As his teacher, she badly wanted him to have the chance to continue his education.

With a few parting words, Mr. Loden inched back down the bench to chat with Annie and Al. Cecily turned to Nick and found him examining her intently, neither smiling nor frowning. "Isn't that exciting?" she exclaimed. "A scout from O.S.U. checking out your nephew!"

"I suppose," Nick granted absently.

Why wasn't he thrilled? she wondered in bemusement. Didn't he want Bruce to succeed? Recalling his impassiveness the last time they'd discussed Bruce's prospects only fed her bewilderment. "How about some bluntness, Nick?" she chided him. "You don't want him to go to college?"

"I didn't say that," he argued. Her steady stare compelled him to continue. "College isn't for everyone, you know," he pointed out. "I want what's best for Bruce, of course I do. But who's to say college is what's best for him?"

"Would you rather he spend the rest of his life wasting away in Glenville?" she challenged Nick.

His lips shaped a grim line as he absorbed her condemning attitude. "I'd rather he decide what's best for himself and then do it. It's not your decision, it's not mine, or his parents' or Mr. Loden's from O.S.U. It's Bruce's life, and I don't want him to feel pressured about it. Maybe college is what he wants, and maybe it isn't. You're the one who says he's got a brain. Let him use it for himself."

The teams returned to the field, and Cecily dropped onto the bench, mulling over what Nick had said. She believed so strongly in the value of a complete education that she'd never given much thought to the possibility that not everyone was destined for college. As a child, she hadn't for a moment doubted that she'd go to college, and her decision to become a teacher was based on her unflagging faith that all young people deserved the kind of education she'd been fortunate enough to receive.

Evidently Nick viewed school differently. She'd grant that maybe not *everyone* ought to go to college, but certainly Bruce ought to go. He had so much potential, and where better to realize that potential than at the state university? To remain forever in Glenville might thwart his chance to make something of himself.

Her vision caught Bruce in play, weaving through a bevy of defenders and snatching the airborne football out of the sky. He made it look so easy, she thought with admiration. His teammates set up for another play which ended in a quarterback sack, negating the yardage Bruce had gained for the team. Cecily cursed.

Hearing her, Nick chuckled. "For a newcomer, you're really taking this game to heart," he teased.

"Well, that was a perfect time for the quarterback to run an option play," she criticized. "They keep running the same three plays. What are they going to do when Bruce graduates? Their entire offense will collapse."

Nick angled his head as he appraised her quizzically. "How do you know so much about it?"

"My husband was a football coach," she answered.

Nick considered her statement. "I thought you said he was a teacher."

She turned to him and nodded. "He taught in the phys-ed department," she explained. "He also coached the football team."

"And you think Doherty stinks compared to him?" Nick guessed.

She smiled. "Frankly, yes."

Nick smiled as well. "Maybe Doherty has less to work with," he suggested. "Smaller budget, torn up field, chintzy salary. He's doing the best he can. Don't be so hard on him."

"You're right," Cecily conceded. "Perhaps I'm being too hard on him." With an impish grin, she added, "Can I help it if I'm infused with that old Glenville school spirit?"

Nick laughed exuberantly and cupped his hand around hers, continuing to hold it for the remainder of the game.

That Glenville ultimately won was a tribute only to Bruce's talent and the opposing team's ineptitude, but Cecily was pleased nonetheless. She and Nick bade farewell to his sister and brother-in-law before working their way through the surge of bodies to the parking lot. "Glenville school spirit," he reflected as he escorted her to his car. "This town's beginning to get to you, huh?"

"Having school spirit is part and parcel of being a good teacher," Cecily commented. "I'd like to think that I'm a good teacher."

"I'm sure you are," said Nick as he unlocked the car. "Maybe if I'd had a teacher like you..." His voice trailing off, he helped her into the bucket seat and closed the door behind her.

She waited until he was settled behind the wheel before inquiring, "If you'd had a teacher like me, what?"

"Maybe I'd have been a better student," he concluded, then disputed himself. "Nah, I'd probably have wound up making goo-goo eyes at you all through class like that moony kid you were fending off yesterday."

"I can't for the life of me imagine you being moony," Cecily chuckled.

"Don't be so sure of it," he argued. "You've already got me pretty moony."

She glanced sharply at him, but his attention was on the traffic feeding out of the lot onto the street. "Are you?" she asked nervously. "Moony about an egghead like me?"

"You were the one who said you weren't an egghead," Nick reminded her. Before she could press him on the more significant issue of his mooniness, he asked, "What made you decide to become a teacher?"

"I loved school as a child," she replied. "And I saw the difference a good teacher could make in a student's life. I'm a firm believer in education."

"You think school's the only place a person can get an education?" Nick asked as the car headed up the incline of Congdon Street.

"I think it's the best place," she declared. "Speaking of education..." She glimpsed the dashboard clock and sighed. "I've got a ton of papers waiting at home for me to grade."

Nick nodded and steered into her apartment complex, coasting to a stop before her building's entry. He switched off the engine. "How about dinner tonight?" he asked.

She hesitated before answering. She'd enjoy having dinner with Nick, but his comment about becoming moony over her unnerved her. She'd spent yesterday evening and much of today with him, and she wanted to spend more time with him. But on more than one occasion during the day he'd offered her clear hints that his feelings for her went beyond the simple enjoyment of being in her company. And she still wasn't certain about her feelings for him.

She liked him, yes, no question about that. She liked him, and she was intrigued by him. She liked the way he flattered her, the way he challenged her. She liked the way his dark, penetrating eyes stirred distinctly feminine responses inside her.

But if she had dinner with him, then what? When would they reach the point they'd reached last night, when those feminine responses threatened to sweep her away and she once again had to face the confusion and doubt that warred within her? How long could she remain with Nick before she was forced to make her own decision about her own life, a decision she wasn't sure she was ready to make?

"No," she whispered meekly, staring through the door's window at her apartment building. "Not tonight."

He reached for her chin and turned her head to face him. "I'm only asking about dinner," he clarified.

"I know," she concurred pensively. "But I also know..."

"That I want you?"

She nodded.

"And that you want me too?"

She wanted him, yes. She wanted to feel his lips taking hers again, and his firm body pressing up to hers. She wanted to feel the stunning sensations she'd felt dancing with him last night. That Nick was an enigma to her, so different from her, from Phil, from every other man she'd ever known, didn't nullify the fact that she wanted him. "I—I need time," she stammered. "I told you, I'm pretty new at this."

"Practice, practice," he muttered with feigned impatience. Then he smiled, another bright, breathtaking smile, and slid his hand to the nape of her neck, drawing her to him. His mouth captured hers, thawed it, softened it to the searing invasion of his tongue.

She lifted her hands to his cheeks, twirling her fingers into the thick black hair at his temples. It felt so good to kiss him, so natural, so right, that she very nearly yielded to her powerful yearning for him. She didn't really need practice, her heart informed her. She'd had six years of practice with Phil. She knew how to fall in love, how to love a man, how to receive a man's love.

Then suddenly Nick was pulling back, releasing her. "Okay, teacher," he whispered hoarsely, letting his fingers drop from her face. "You need time—you got it." His hand shook slightly as he pulled the lever to open his door. By the time he'd reached her side of the car he'd regained control of himself. "A few sleepless nights won't kill me," he joked away his disappointment.

Cecily wondered what effect a few more nights like the previous night would have on her. Yet she silently thanked him for his willpower, for backing off before she could give in to the imperative desire that raged through her. She *did* need time, and she was infinitely grateful to Nick for allowing her to take it.

Four

I'm giving you a few days off," Nick said Sunday morning.

Cecily tossed her red pen onto the pile of papers she'd been grading and brushed a heavy lock of chestnut hair away from her ear with her hand so she could hear him more clearly through the telephone receiver. The sound of his voice was now familiar, its husky rumble stroking her nerves and awakening them more effectively than the two cups of black coffee she'd consumed upon arising.

"A few days off?" she asked.

"That's right. I've got to fly down to St. Louis this afternoon to meet with some people Monday—and probably on into the week. Business. I'm not sure how long I'll be gone, but I'll be out of your hair for a few days, lucky you."

Cecily didn't think there was anything so lucky about having Nick out of her hair for a few days. She was unable to deny that his leaving Glenville would offer her the needed opportunity to think through what was going on between her and Nick, and to come to terms with what she *wanted* to be going on between them. But an irrational sadness twisted through her at the realization that she wouldn't see him for a while. He wasn't yet gone and already she missed him.

She couldn't tell him that, though. His willingness to give her time to work through her emotions was one of the things she liked best about him. She couldn't very well complain about his doing exactly what she wanted him to do. Instead, she said, "Pretty short notice for a business trip, isn't it?"

"My partner was supposed to make the trip," Nick explained. "But he called this morning to say his wife had the flu—nothing serious, but since they've got two kids he doesn't want to be so far from home while his wife's under the weather."

"He sounds like a very sweet man," Cecily observed.

"Yeah, for a snob," Nick countered, his gentle laugh conveying that he was joking. "I don't think there's anything so sweet about my having to bury myself in St. Louis for days. I've got to convince some turkey that even though another outfit underbid us on a job we ought to get the job because we offer better quality." He sighed, and his voice held no hint of teasing when he added, "Believe me, I'd much rather be here with you."

His compliment washed through Cecily, warming her, causing her cheeks to redden. She'd never imagined herself particularly susceptible to flattery, but whenever Nick complimented her she was keenly aware of the sincerity in his words. When he told her she had the most gorgeous figure he'd ever seen, she knew he wasn't simply handing her a line. And when he confessed that he'd rather be in Glenville with her than in St. Louis on business, she knew he meant it.

Again she wrestled with the urge to give voice to her feelings, to tell him she wanted him to stay here with her, to admit that she'd miss him when he left. "I'm sorry you have to go, Nick," was as far as she would commit herself.

She could almost feel his smile through the telephone wire. "Are you saying that to be polite?" he asked.

"No, I'm saying that to be blunt."

He laughed softly. "In that case, save Friday evening for me. I should be home by then."

"Friday evening," she echoed. "You're on."

"As a matter of fact, I should be off. I've got to get packed and on my way. I'll give you a call from St. Louis once I have an idea when I'll be back, okay?"

"Okay. Good luck, Nick."

He snorted. "I don't need luck, Cecily. O.R.'s better than our competitor. We'll win the job. All it'll take is holding a few people's hands and walking them through the situation until they see things my way. Take care—I'll see you Friday."

"Have a good trip," Cecily said before lowering the receiver. She crossed to her coffee pot and refilled her cup, then carried it to the kitchen table, where a few remaining student essays waited for her to attack them with her red pen. Dropping onto her chair, she took a sip of coffee and reached for the pen.

Staring at the essay before her, she found herself unable to concentrate. Her mind wandered to Nick, to his boastful parting comment about not needing luck. He was so proud, proud of his company, his town, his accomplishments. Yet she didn't find his arrogance offensive. Pride was simply a part of what made him what he was. Pride, confidence, candor, his piercing dark eyes, his tall, lean build...

His willpower. She set down the pen and sighed. No longer did she wonder whether she was responding to Nick himself or simply to his being a man. He hadn't yet left Glenville, but the thought of his impending absence filled her with an unexpected sense of desolation. If he were just a man, she wouldn't mind that he'd be gone for a few days. She'd endured almost two years without male companionship; a few days wouldn't make much difference.

But Nick wasn't male companionship. He was...he was Nick, an individual, a man she cared for, the first man since Phil who dared to touch her heart and inhabit her soul. She'd come to recognize her feelings the day before. Perhaps not consciously, but somehow she'd known the truth yesterday when he'd kissed her in his car. She'd been ready to invite him inside her home, to allow him to love her fully. Only his willpower had prevented her from taking that step. He, not Cecily, had been the one to break away, to remind her that she needed time and that he'd provide her with it. And for one fleeting moment, when he'd turned from her and reached for the doorlatch with a trembling hand, she'd seen his arrogance and certainty slipping, revealing a glimpse of his own confusion and doubt.

She wondered whether he regretted having pulled back from her yesterday just when she was on the verge of succumbing to the passion that flared between them. She wondered whether he usually practiced such restraint around women. She wondered whether he expected his patience to be ultimately rewarded with the ultimate reward. She didn't think so; Nick Faro didn't seem the type who designed his behavior around some self-gratifying goal he hoped to achieve in return for his efforts.

"Enough of this woolgathering," she scolded herself as she lifted the pen and tackled a student essay. She wouldn't be seeing Nick for nearly a week. She certainly couldn't spend that week frittering away her time daydreaming about him. She had work to do, and with a resolute shrug, she shoved him from her thoughts and focused on the paper to be graded.

Nick might have been shoved from Cecily's thoughts, but he hadn't been shoved from her students' thoughts in her senior Government systems class Monday morning. She lugged the carton of essays into the classroom and dropped it onto her desk with a definitive thud, but before she could lecture the class on the overall quality of the essays, a boy at the back of the room shouted, "Hey, Mrs. Adams, have you got a boyfriend?"

Her eyes flashed a brilliant green towards the nosy boy, and then towards another boy seated a row to the left who punctuated the first boy's comment with a strident wolf-whistle. Of course, when she'd approached Nick last week in the school's parking lot and called him "sweetheart," she'd intended the existence of her "boyfriend" to become public knowledge around the school. But now that her relationship with Nick had transcended play-acting, she found the student's remark disconcerting.

She wondered whether Richard Pettibone had instigated a telephone tree just to spread the gossip on Cecily's social life through Glenville. That wasn't likely; Richard was too shy. Rather than let the boy in the back row know that he'd rattled her, however, she let her lips slide into a relaxed grin and asked, "Where did you hear that?"

"I didn't hear it, I saw it," the boy replied. "You were with him at the game Saturday. Holding hands."

This announcement was met with several giggles and another wolf-whistle. Cecily's gaze skimmed the room, and she spotted Bruce Munsey slouching in his chair—trying to crawl beneath it, she surmised, as she read the discomfort in his lopsided grin. Perhaps his classmates had already kidded him mercilessly about his uncle's having taken up with the school's new social studies teacher. She offered him an apologetic smile and then turned back to her taunter in the back row. "If you want my opinion, Steve," she said coolly, "you would have been better off skipping the football game last Saturday and using the time to read the dictionary. Judging from your last paper, I have the distinct impression that spelling isn't exactly your long suit."

More jeers and titters engulfed the room, but this time they were directed at the boy in the back row instead of at Cecily. She was easily able to steer the discussion to the papers as a whole.

She maintained firm control of the class until the bell rang to end it. As the students filed through the door and out of the room, she caught Bruce's eye and signalled for him to stay. She wanted to tell him that her dating Nick had nothing to do with him, and that he shouldn't feel awkward about it. But as he fidgeted with his notebook and then raked one of his beefy hands through his sandy colored hair, he looked so abashed that she couldn't think of a tactful way to bring up the subject.

She peered up at him, a huge hulk of a boy, his neck and thighs thickened by exercise and his face favoring the pleasant features of his father. "Bruce," she began, struggling to sound objective. "You played very well on Saturday."

He nodded in thanks and pretended to be fascinated by the blackboard behind Cecily.

"I understand you're being courted by Ohio State University."

His eyes met hers, an inkling of interest illuminating them. "Yeah, that's right."

"Well, Bruce, you probably think it's none of my business, but as your teacher, I want you to know that I think you'd do quite well at the university. You're a bright boy with a lot of potential. Your essay would have received a B or an A if you'd taken a little more time with it, paced

yourself, and didn't rush through it. I'm speaking as your
teacher, Bruce, not as—as a friend of your uncle's,'' she
managed, hoping to persuade him that her hopes for his
future had nothing to do with Nick. ''I'd love to see you
make a go of it at O.S.U. If there's anything I can do to help,
please let me know.''

He studied her, and the intense glow of his eyes was
sharply reminiscent of Nick's eyes, despite their different
coloring. Bruce weighed what she'd said, then cracked a
modest smile. ''You think I'm bright?'' he asked. At her
nod, he laughed. ''Coach Doherty says all they care about
at O.S.U. is how well I can catch a pass.''

''That may be true,'' Cecily agreed. ''But once you're in,
you can get yourself a fine education. That's what college
is supposed to be about.''

''Yeah, well…'' He shrugged. ''I don't know. They
haven't accepted me or anything yet, so…'' He shrugged
again, then started toward the door. ''Thanks for saying I'm
bright,'' he called over his shoulder.

''Oh, Bruce?'' she shouted after him. He paused in the
doorway and pivoted around to face her. ''Tell Coach
Doherty to try a screen play one of these days. The offense
could use some versatility.''

Bruce's surprised smile indicated more respect for Cecily
than he'd ever shown before. ''Yeah, I keep telling him
that,'' he concurred. ''Maybe you ought to lay it out for him
at the next faculty meeting or something.''

''I'll do that,'' Cecily promised. She waved Bruce out into
the bustling corridor, then organized her notes and slid them
into her briefcase. The following period was a free one for
her, and she left her classroom for the faculty lounge on the
ground floor.

Entering the dimly lit room, she immediately spotted
Gary Czymanski puffing on a cigarette. He beckoned her to

join him on the tattered sofa, and after filling a styrofoam cup with coffee from the machine beneath the window, Cecily took a seat next to him. "You ought to quit smoking," she said by way of greeting.

Gary took her criticism in stride. "I'll quit smoking if you'll quit wearing clothes," he suggested.

"Wearing clothes won't give me cancer," she argued.

"Who's to say?" Gary sniffed. "I guarantee that within five years the scientific establishment is going to announce that pantyhose causes tumors in rats."

"Rats deserve tumors," Cecily commented dryly. "Although I've never seen a rat wearing stockings."

Gary twisted on the cracked vinyl surface of the couch to confront Cecily. "The hell with rats," he declared. "I'm a desperate man. Maybe you can help me."

"Help you with what?"

"I'm the chairman of next week's career assembly." At Cecily's blank stare, he elaborated, "A couple of times a year the school holds a career assembly for the upperclassmen. We have three speakers with three different jobs, and each one speaks about his or her work and background and answers questions. The kids find these things informative—or at least they're happy for the excuse to get out of a couple of classes in the afternoon. The assemblies are usually a success."

"Then why are you a desperate man?" Cecily asked.

"One of my speakers cancelled out on me," he revealed, pulling out another cigarette and lighting it. "I've got a dentist and a woman who does something with computers at Glenville Central Bank, but my third speaker was supposed to be a fellow who owns his own realty concern. He backed out on me last week, and I've got until a week from Friday to find a replacement. I've been on the phone all weekend trying to scrounge someone up, but no luck. Can you help me out?"

"Gary, I'm new in town, remember? How am I supposed to know anyone who might want to speak at an assembly?"

"I told you I was desperate," Gary muttered with mock dismay. "If I wasn't, do you think I'd ask you for help?"

Cecily sipped her coffee and mused. "Are you looking for someone in a particular kind of business?" she asked.

He shook his head. "The way we work it, we usually try to get one professional, one employee of a large company like the bank, and one entrepreneur. Kind of a balanced panel. Help me out, Cecily—can you think of any owner-run business led by someone who'd make a good speaker for the kids? I've asked everyone in our department, and most of them have come up with speakers who've already turned me down."

"Can't you have just two speakers this time?" Cecily asked.

"Three's better," Gary insisted.

Cecily ruminated for a moment. She didn't know many people in Glenville at all, but she did happen to know one entrepreneur, a man who had founded and now ran his own successful business. She was certain Nick would make a splendid speaker at the high school, since he was a loyal local resident with tremendous affection for his home town and great pride in his accomplishments. But would he want to speak to a student assembly? She'd have to ask him before she mentioned his name to Gary. "I've got someone in mind," she hedged. "Let me talk to him first, okay?"

"Beg him," Gary pleaded. "Twist his arm. Offer him your body. I'm *desperate*, Cecily."

"If you're so desperate, why don't *you* offer him *your* body?" she commented with a smile. "Write down the date and time for me, Gary, and I'll talk to him when I can. But I'm promising nothing, you understand."

Gary jotted the information down for Cecily and pressed the slip of paper into her hand. "I feel five degrees less desperate already," he said, presenting her with a grateful smile.

Nick sounded lukewarm when Cecily described the assembly to him over the phone Tuesday evening. "Are they still holding those Career Day things?" he groaned. "They used to have them when I was at Glenville High. The most boring assemblies in the world."

"If you spoke," Cecily pointed out, "you could make sure it didn't get boring."

He still didn't seem terribly enthusiastic, and Cecily decided to let the subject drop until she saw him on Friday. She was sure that in person she could convince him of what an honor it would be to address students, to inspire them, to prove what a young Glenville man with intelligence and courage could achieve. If she couldn't convince him during a static-riddled long-distance call from St. Louis, it wasn't the end of the world.

Nick concluded the brief call by telling her that he'd be arriving back in Glenville late Thursday night. He'd pick her up at her apartment Friday at six.

"I'm afraid to ask what I should wear," she remarked impishly.

"You already know what I'll answer, so don't bother asking," Nick parried. "I'll see you Friday."

When Cecily awoke Friday morning, she felt out of sorts. She'd gone to bed the previous night feeling exhilarated, astoundingly joyful about Nick's return to Glenville and their impending date. She hadn't known what sort of evening he had in mind for them—dinner at a snobby restaurant or at Darlene's, the back-alley diner with the big portions and the small prices—or of what might occur after dinner. But she did know that she wanted to see Nick, wanted to be with him, wanted him with her. That was all that mattered Thursday night.

But now, as she sat up and tried to rub the sleep out of her eyes, she felt not joyful but queasy. Her head ached, her hands were chilly, her stomach seemed to be tied in enough knots to win her a Boy Scout merit badge.

Maybe she had the flu, she wondered glumly. If Nick's partner's wife had the flu, perhaps it was making the rounds, infecting everyone in the Heights. Cecily didn't feel feverish, though, or nauseous. Just vaguely queasy. Something wasn't right.

Groaning, she swung her feet over the edge of the bed and stared blearily at her alarm clock. She stood, and her legs wobbled beneath her. What in the world was wrong with her? she fumed. The light filtering through her translucent voile drapes hinted at a glorious sun-filled day. Nick was home, the weekend loomed ahead with two free days, no papers to grade, nothing hanging over her head...

And then it struck her with all the force of a sledge hammer slamming into her solar plexus. October 20th. Today. Exactly two years ago today a police officer had appeared on her doorstep and said, "I'm afraid I have some bad news."

Her knees began to quake, and she dropped back onto the mattress. She didn't have the strength to hold back the wrenching sob that swelled up from her chest. She'd done a decent job of overcoming her anguish during the past two years, but today, on this grimmest of anniversaries, the pain and grief of losing Phil swamped her, beating relentlessly down upon her, crushing her.

She wept freely, venting the pain and sorrow she'd managed to contain for so long. Today it couldn't be suppressed; today she couldn't fight it. She surrendered, letting the sobs wrack her body, unleashing the hatred she felt for the driver who'd caused the accident, the crazed hatred she felt for Phil for having died on her when she loved him so much.

After a while her tears were spent, but she still felt awful. Her bones seemed oddly fragile, her skeleton barely able to support her flesh. Her head continued to throb.

Dabbing at her cheeks, she trudged to the kitchen and dialed the high school's number. A secretary answered, and Cecily told the woman she wouldn't be coming to work. "I seem to have caught a bug," she fibbed, unwilling to reveal the actual reason for her distraught condition to the secretary. Her voice feeble and cracking, she listed the day's class assignments for the secretary to pass along to a substitute teacher. After thanking the secretary for her expressed wish that Cecily feel better, she hung up.

A fresh spate of tears filled her eyes, and she sank onto a chair and covered her face with her palms. She wept, her chest tormented by shuddering spasms, her throat becoming raw. "I'm sorry, Mrs. Adams, I'm afraid I have some bad news..." The policeman's voice echoed inside her skull, reverberating until she thought she'd scream.

Eventually the convulsive sobs stopped. She took several deep breaths to steady herself, then moved back to her bedroom to put on her bathrobe. She was amazed that her sorrow could seize her so unexpectedly, just when her life seemed to be coming back together, just when her spirit seemed ready to blossom again. Anniversaries, she realized, were occasions for remembering, even when one wanted only to forget.

She wouldn't be able to see Nick tonight, not feeling the way she did. She was in no mood to be charming, pleasant, amorous. Today was a day to spend alone, reflecting, remembering, recovering all over again.

Returning to the kitchen, she pulled her telephone directory from its shelf and thumbed through it until she found the listing for O.R. Enterprises. She dialed the number, then tried to rub feeling back into her frigid fingertips as she listened to the phone ringing on the other end. A receptionist answered: "O.R. Enterprises, good morning."

"May I speak to Nick Faro please? This is Cecily Adams."

The receptionist put her on hold. In less than a minute, Nick was on the line. "Cecily? Hi, what's up?"

The sound of his voice conjured his image in her mind, his virile physique, his intriguing eyes, the inherent strength in his arms. She was gripped by an illogical longing to feel those arms wrapped tightly around her, holding her, comforting her. She smothered the longing, knowing that she couldn't expect Nick to comfort her now. She had no right to want such a thing. She had to be strong, to pull herself together without assistance. Phil's death was her tragedy, not Nick's.

She swallowed and prayed for her voice to hold. "I'm afraid I can't see you tonight," she said.

"You sound horrible," Nick observed compassionately. "What's wrong?"

"I—I might be coming down with something," she mumbled. She didn't want to lie to him, but she couldn't bear the possibility that if she told him the truth he might pity her for it. "I've got a terrible headache, and I'm all stuffed up," she added. At least that was the truth.

"Are you home now?" he asked.

"Yes, I'm taking the day off."

"Have you called a doctor?"

"Oh, I don't think it's that bad," Cecily assured him, sounding much more certain than she felt. "I think it'll blow over on its own."

Nick deferred to her judgment. "Okay. Get into bed and sleep it off. I'll give you a call tomorrow to see how you're doing."

"Thanks, Nick. Don't worry, it's really nothing to be concerned about. I'm sure I'll be all right in a few days."

"Okay," he said again. "Take care of yourself—I'll be in touch."

Hanging up the phone, she felt her legs growing wobbly again. She stumbled to the living room and collapsed onto the sofa. She felt frail, unbelievably weak. Even her hair seemed too heavy, weighing uncomfortably on her shoulders and back.

Her mother would advise her to give in to her sadness, to wallow in it. Cecily wouldn't do that, though. She'd spent months upon months rebuilding herself, and she wasn't going to let this one ghastly day undo everything she'd achieved in two years.

With a determination that had seen her through many bleak, torturous days, she stood and strode to her bedroom closet. On a shelf above the hanger rod sat her wedding album. She pulled down the bulky white book and settled on her bed. Gritting her teeth, she opened it.

She had looked at the album enough times to know each photograph by heart. There was Phil, his large, athletic body filling out his tuxedo and his arm curved snugly about his bride. And there he was again, wedged with her between her parents and his, and there, laughing as his best man made a wedding toast, and there, dancing with Cecily, the entire dance floor belonging to them and them alone. She recalled that first dance with Phil, the magical privacy she'd felt with him in a reception room crowded with family and friends. She'd felt as if only he existed, only his marvellous smile and his muscular body pressed up to hers. That memory was abruptly supplanted by a memory of her first dance with Nick, in which she'd felt the very same sensation, that she and he were alone in the world, alone and together. Startled by the thought, she flipped the page.

It hurt to look at the pictures. It hurt to see Phil so alive, so animated, with his broad, toothy grin, his thick, slightly unkempt blond hair, his grace despite the powerful dimensions of his build. Although he hadn't played organized football since his college days, he'd kept himself in magnificent shape, and even at the ripe old age of thirty-two, he'd been as swift and agile as his youthful charges. It hurt Cecily to see him, to remember, but she believed that if she could survive the hurt, she'd be strong again.

She wasn't aware of how long she sat on the bed, staring at the photographs. When her doorbell rang, she glanced at her alarm clock and was shocked to discover that it was after twelve.

Combing her fingers through her hair and shrugging her robe tightly about herself, she stalked to the front door and answered it. A wiry young man stood in the hall, holding a single red rose and a small paper bag. "This is from Mr. Faro," he announced, passing the items to her. "He said to tell you to eat it while it's hot." Before Cecily could speak, the man spun on his heel and jogged to the stairway and out of sight.

Frowning, she closed the door and carried the bag and the rose to the kitchen. She opened the bag and found a cardboard container and a folded note. Unfolding it, she read: "Good for what ails you—Nick." She pried off the lid and found the container filled with steaming minestrone soup.

For the first time all day, she smiled. She knew that chicken soup was the supposed cure for colds, not minestrone—but maybe Nick had intuited that what ailed Cecily wasn't a cold. A lovely rose and hot soup were probably the best treatment for what ailed her.

She filled a crystal bud vase with water and set the rose in it, then located a spoon. She managed to swallow two mouthfuls of the rich soup before her throat choked with tears again. It was unfair for her to let Nick think she was actually ill. He was so kind, so generous, so thoughtful. His gesture was so sweet... She had to tell him the truth. She couldn't lie to him.

Rising from the table, she reached for the telephone and dialed his firm's number. As before, the receptionist put through her call at once. "Hello, Cecily," Nick greeted her. "Did you finish your soup like a good girl?"

"No," she admitted, futilely trying to smooth the catch in her voice.

"Hey, children are starving in Africa," he reminded her. "And you can't ship soup in the mails, so you've got to eat it yourself."

"Nick," she interrupted his playful words. "Nick, I'm not sick."

He hesitated before responding. "Oh?"

"I'm not feeling too good, Nick, but it's nothing that soup can cure," she forged ahead. "Today..." She inhaled and forced herself to continue. "When I woke up today I realized that it was October 20th. That's the day my husband died, Nick, two years ago today, and..." She sighed. "I just fell apart, that's all."

He said nothing for a long moment. Then, "I don't think there's any rule against that. You should have told me the truth this morning."

"I know," Cecily said contritely. "But—I guess I was embarrassed. I didn't want you to pity me."

"I don't pity you, Cecily," he murmured. "That ought to be obvious by now."

"Yes," she said genuinely. "It means a lot to me that you don't."

"Let me see you tonight," he requested. "We don't have to go out or anything. Just let me come over and give you a hug, and then I'll be on my way if you want to be alone."

The tears that filled her eyes now arose not from pain or misery but from relief, relief that someone as sensitive and kind as Nick had entered her life. She felt immeasurably lucky to have him as a friend. "Come," she said softly. "Come and hug me."

"I'll get there when I can," he promised. "I'll leave work early and come straight over. And in the meantime, you'd better eat your soup."

Cecily didn't eat her soup; she didn't have any appetite. But her spirits improved as she waited for Nick. She took a shower and dressed, brushed her hair, and perked up her drawn face with some light make-up. A hug from Nick would cure what his soup couldn't.

He arrived at her apartment shortly before five, dressed in a slightly rumpled blue suit with his tie loosened and his collar unbuttoned. Before entering the living room he gave Cecily a lengthy inspection. In spite of her attempts to make herself presentable, he couldn't help noticing the shadows under her eyes, her wan complexion, the tension tugging down the corners of her mouth.

He stepped across the threshold and, as promised, he gave her a bracing hug. His arms felt wonderful around her, and she rested her head on his shoulder, absorbing his strength and feeling it infuse her. "How are you doing?" he whispered into her hair.

"I'm glad you're here," she murmured softly.

He released her and shut the door behind him. Then he shed his blazer and tossed it over the back of a chair. He kicked off his loafers and headed directly to the kitchen. His eyes rested for a moment on the solitary rose displayed at the center of her table, and his lips curved in a gentle smile. The smile faded as he swung open the refrigerator door and found the nearly untouched container of soup on a shelf. "You were supposed to eat this," he scolded her. "What's the matter, you don't like soup?"

"It was delicious," Cecily defended herself. "I had a little."

"Very little," he estimated, opening the container and frowning. "I'm going to heat it up for you now."

"I'm really not hungry," she protested.

"When was the last time you ate?" he posed. Her answering silence caused his frown to deepen, and he rummaged through her cabinets until he found a pot. He dumped the container's contents into it and set it on the stove.

"You must be hungry yourself," Cecily guessed. "Why don't you eat the soup?"

He glared at her, then opened her refrigerator again and surveyed its contents. "I'll rustle up something," he muttered. "The soup's for you." He discovered a loaf of whole-wheat bread and jars of peanut butter and grape jelly. "Fix me a drink and we'll call this dinner," he resolved as he bent to the task of preparing sandwiches.

Cecily moved to the cabinet where she kept her liquor. "I haven't got any bourbon," she apologized, remembering the drink he'd ordered when they'd gone out to dinner.

"Give me what you've got. I'm not fussy."

She mixed them both scoth-and-sodas and carried the glasses to the table. Once Nick was done making his sand-

wiches he poured the hot soup into a bowl and set it before
Cecily.

They didn't talk over dinner. Cecily gamefully consumed
the tasty soup even though she had to force herself. Nick
wolfed down his two sandwiches with gusto, and she resolved that someday soon she'd make him a real dinner,
something hearty enough to fill his lanky, energetic body.

When they were through cleaning up from their meal,
Nick slid his arms around Cecily and kissed her forehead.
"Do you want me to go?" he asked, his tone implying that
he'd accept her decision without argument.

But she didn't want him to go. She'd spent the entire day
alone, lost in thought, talking to herself. Nick's presence
boosted her spirits, and she didn't want to revert to the
soppy, mopey person she'd been all day. "Stay," she said.

Smiling with satisfaction, he took their empty glasses to
the counter and mixed two fresh drinks. Then he led her to
the living room. They sat side by side on the sofa, Nick
arching one arm around Cecily's shoulders and urging her
to lean comfortably against him. "Do you want to talk?"
he asked.

"About what?"

"About anything." His fingers ravelled through her hair
as he studied his drink. "Why don't you tell me about
him?"

For some reason, the question didn't surprise her. She
realized that she *did* want to tell Nick about Phil, to tell him
about herself, her past, the marriage that had been such a
vital part of her life. "His name was Phil," she began in a
muted voice. "He was a football coach."

"You told me that," Nick reminded her, tucking her head
more snugly against his shoulder.

She nodded. "He was a fantastic man, Nick. Big and
blond, very physical in appearance. And personality," she

added. "He ate like a horse—or like a football player, I suppose. I had to watch what I ate all the time, and he could pack it away and burn it off without blinking. I used to resent the hell out of him for being able to indulge his sweet tooth without a moment's pause." She smiled. It felt good to talk this way, to share Phil with Nick. "He was an excellent coach."

"Better than Doherty," Nick chuckled.

"Much better. He was so good to his boys, Nick, so concerned about them. He didn't care about whether they won as much as whether they were good sports. Before each game..." She laughed as she reminisced. "He'd never lead the boys in a pre-game prayer. He used to say, 'God has more important things to deal with than whether or not we win this game. So let's win it on our own and save our prayers for things like world peace and feeding the hungry.'"

Her smile softened as her memories drifted. They no longer hurt as they'd hurt all day. Remembering didn't have to be painful when Nick was present to console her, to listen. "He used to organize the team to visit the children's wing at the local hospital each year," she recalled. "They'd play with the kids, sing songs, cheer them up. Phil believed it was good for his athletes to be reminded that being strong and healthy was a special blessing. He was...he was more than a coach, Nick. He was a teacher in the most basic sense of the word. He taught his boys what life was all about, and how they could get the most out of it by giving the most."

Nick reflected on what Cecily had told him. "He sounds great."

"He was. You'd have liked him," she murmured. "He was very funny, too. He had a bizarre sense of humor. He loved to tease me."

"About what?" Nick asked.

"You name it," Cecily groaned. "He used to tease me about grading my students too harshly, and about taking the faculty meetings too seriously. He used to tease me about being too neat around the house. He used to leave his socks everywhere. All these ribbed sweatsocks on the sofa, on the dining room table, on top of the television set. I'd always yell at him, and then he'd tease me. He'd call me the 'sock-it-to-me' lady." She laughed. "He used to tease me about being a prude."

"Are you?"

She pulled away from Nick's shoulder in order to see his face. She hadn't intended to reveal anything that personal about her relationship with Phil, but the words had spilled out quite naturally, and Nick's tantalizing grin erased her embarrassment about having said what she did. "Not really," she answered truthfully. "I'm just a bit more reserved than he was. I like to be very sure of things before I take the plunge."

"Hmm," Nick grunted, his grin expanding. "So I've noticed."

She felt her own smile waning as she assessed him. "Does it bother you, Nick?" she asked earnestly. "I mean, that I've—that I haven't—?"

He silenced her with a light kiss. "I don't want you to plunge into anything you aren't sure of," he swore. "You'll be sure of me in time, Cecily. I'm positive about that."

"You're a very confident man," Cecily commented, nestling back against his shoulder.

"Maybe I have a right to be," Nick responded, weaving his fingers through her hair again.

Cecily closed her eyes and relaxed in his embrace. Yes, she thought, the muscles in her neck and shoulders melting beneath his gentle caresses. Nick was confident, and he certainly had a right to be.

Five

The sunlight spilling in a hazy stream through her drawn bedroom curtains roused Cecily. She opened her eyes, stretched languorously, and sat up in bed. Discovering herself fully clothed and lying on top of her blanket perplexed her, and she frowned as she tried to figure out how she'd wound up in bed.

The last thing she remembered was sitting with Nick on her couch, sipping a drink and telling him about Phil. And then snuggling up to him, curling her body cozily against his like a contented kitten...She must have drifted off in his arms.

The realization didn't embarrass her. What could Nick have expected, when he'd managed to make her feel so comfortable and relaxed with him? Especially after the day she'd lived yesterday—the emotional rollercoaster she'd ridden had exhausted her, and two tall scotch-and-sodas were more than she usually consumed.

She wasn't embarrassed, but rather touched, touched by
the image of Nick letting her doze against his shoulder, then
lifting her off the sofa carrying her to bed. What a fine man
he was, she thought as she brushed her hair back from her
sleep-warm cheeks. His mere presence yesterday evening had
worked on her like a magic elixir, vanquishing all the de-
mons she'd been fighting. The misery she'd suffered
throughout the day was gone. Nick had chased it away.

Smiling, she heaved herself off the bed and stretched
again. Her clock read nearly nine-thirty. She wondered how
long she'd been sleeping.

She hadn't opened her drapes yesterday, but today she
pulled them back to let the sunlight into her room, back into
her life. Yesterday she'd wrapped herself in gloom, but yesterday was past. Today she wanted sunshine.

She padded in her socks down the hall to the living room,
eager to open those drapes as well, to march out onto her
terrace and breathe some fresh air. But at the entrance to the
living room she halted.

Nick was asleep on her sofa. His tall body extended across
three wide sections, and even at that his feet hung over the
side. His jacket and tie were draped neatly over a chair, his
shoes placed side by side on the carpet next to it.

She studied his slumbering form. She'd never really appreciated how long his legs were before. The navy blue wool
of his trousers matched the blue fabric of the sofa. Indeed,
she pondered, he went with her furniture much better than
her furniture went with the apartment. He looked like he
belonged here.

His hair drooped across his forehead, and his cheeks were
shadowed by an overnight growth of beard. The tempta-
tion to push back his hair, to kiss his peaceful lips, was too
great to resist. Cecily tiptoed to his side, lowered herself onto
the edge of the sofa's cushion, and wove her fingers into the

thick black silk covering his temples. Timidly she touched her mouth to his.

His eyes fluttered open. They took a moment to focus, and he smiled. "What an incredible sight to wake up to," he whispered hoarsely, sliding his hand to the back of her head and drawing her lips to his.

His kiss was startlingly provocative, given his drowsy state, and as soon as he released Cecily she straightened up, flustered by her instantaneous response to him. "Nick," she murmured, letting her hand drop from his head to his shoulder. He immediately folded his own hand around it, holding it in place. "Nick, why did you spend the night on the sofa?"

He chuckled. "I may have my faults, Cecily, but give me some credit. I don't take advantage of sleeping women."

Coloring slightly, she laughed. "No, I mean, why didn't you go home?"

His smile faded as he studied her face above his. "I didn't want to leave you alone last night," he told her. "You might have awakened in the middle of the night and needed to talk some more, or cry some more...I thought I ought to stick around, just in case."

"Oh, Nick..." Her voice evaporated before she could think of the words that would describe what she was feeling. How could she tell him how much his kindness meant to her, how moved she was by his solicitude...Was there any way to express her gratitude, her pleasure at having him with her?

There was, and her body showed her the way. She bowed down to him again, covering his mouth with hers. His arms circled her, holding her close, accepting the unspoken message she was communicating.

Their tongues met and he groaned. He guided her fully up onto the sofa, arranging her body on top of his, wedging one of his legs between hers. As his kiss grew more demanding, he let one hand float down her back to her waist, to her hips, pressing her to him as he stirred beneath her. While her mind acknowledged his sudden readiness her flesh matched him in eagerness, receptively mirroring his sensuous rhythm as he moved against her. Her hands dug into his hair, clinging to his head as his mouth slid from hers to kiss her cheeks, chin, and throat.

What might not have been right before was definitely right at this moment, she knew. She no longer worried about her response to Nick; she no longer questioned what she felt for him. Her time of mourning had ended the moment he appeared in her life, and now she was finally ready to admit that truth.

Her fingers drifted to his chest, opening two buttons of his shirt to explore his skin. He groaned again, drawing his hands forward to capture her breasts. "Cecily," he whispered, apparently engaged in mental debate even as he toured her sensitive flesh through her blouse and then centered his thumbs on her swollen nipples. "Cecily, we can't do this." With great effort he let his hands fall to the upholstery and closed his eyes.

She stared at him, puzzled. "Nick, it's...this is..." She swallowed, fighting against her uneven breath as much as her disappointment and bewilderment at his sudden withdrawal. "I *am* sure of this, Nick."

He opened his eyes again and laughed, then shook his head. "What I meant to say," he explained, cupping his hand consolingly about her chin, "is that I've got to get to work. It must be late."

"It's nine-thirty," she informed him.

His grin dissolving into a grimace, he cursed. He eased Cecily into a sitting position and wiggled his legs out from under her. "It's late," he grumbled.

"It's Saturday."

"And I was gone all week, and I left work early yester-day," he reminded her. "You don't want to know how much stuff is sitting on my desk waiting for me. Being a boss-man ain't all it's cracked up to be." He stood, extended his hand to Cecily, and helped her to her feet. "Believe me, Cecily, this hurts me more than it hurts you," he swore, folding his arms around her shoulders and drawing her into a tight hug. His lips grazed her brow, the bridge of her nose and its tip, and he resolutely pulled back again. "Tonight," he prom-ised.

Tonight. Cecily's mind was branded by the single word. Tonight she would be Nick's, and he hers. Tonight she would become a whole woman again. She'd waited two years. She could wait a few hours more. That would be far preferable to racing against the clock this morning when Nick was preoccupied by the responsibilities awaiting him at his office.

Nodding, she smiled sheepishly and tucked her shirt smoothly into her jeans. "Do you want any breakfast be-fore you go?" she asked.

"That I won't refuse," said Nick.

She strode into the kitchen, calling over her shoulder, "It probably won't be as good as that feast we ate at Dar-lene's."

"I'm easy to please," he called back to her.

She prepared a pot of coffee, and while it was brewing she scrambled some eggs and popped a couple of slices of bread into the toaster. She heard Nick heading down the hall to the bathroom. By the time the first batch of toast was brown and the eggs nearly cooked, he joined her in the kitchen, his shirt once again buttoned and his tie looped through the collar. "Why is it," he complained as he rubbed his bristly jaw, "that ladies always have flimsy pink razors?"

"Maybe because they use those razors on their flimsy pink legs," she returned, nudging him into a chair. She set two glasses of orange juice on the table, then served the eggs. "Don't you have time to stop off at home and shave?" she asked.

He shrugged. "I'm not going to be seeing anyone I've got to impress today," he said nonchalantly. "More times than not I go to work wearing jeans. By now most of the people I work with know I'm a bum."

Cecily chuckled as she buttered her toast. Raising it to her mouth, she paused to study the man across the table from her. His eyes were dark and warm, and she recalled for a moment how sweet and shimmering they'd looked when he was still half asleep. "How old are you?" she asked.

He lifted his gaze to her and quirked his left eyebrow upward. "Thirty-six," he answered. "Why do you ask?"

"I was just wondering how someone like you managed to stay unattached all these years."

He laughed. "Fancy footwork," he joked. "Actually, I've had a couple of close calls."

"Oh?" Cecily's face radiated curiosity.

Nick obliged her with an explanation. "The first one was a girl I was involved with when I was a kid. Then I got drafted and did my time, and when I came home I found out she was already married to someone else."

"Ouch," Cecily grunted.

Nick waved off her concern. "If she was that fickle, I guess she wouldn't have made much of a wife for me," he mused. "It was kind of a shock, but in retrospect I think she did a pretty decent thing by keeping her marriage a secret from me while I was in 'Nam. She told me she didn't want to send me a 'Dear John,' because she was afraid I might become so upset I'd do something crazy and get myself hurt. All in all, I've got to thank her for that."

Cecily nodded. "How about the second close call?"

Nick sipped his coffee, reminiscing. "That was a few years ago. She was a nurse at Glenville General. A terrific lady."

"What happened?"

He drained his cup, and Cecily carried it to the counter for a refill. "She had a dream about moving to California," he related. "It had been a life-long fantasy of hers. One day the opportunity to move there cropped up for her. O.R. was still pretty shaky in those days, but making a go of it here in Glenville was my dream. I guess our dreams didn't jibe. That's just the way it goes sometimes."

Cecily wondered whether Nick loved Glenville more than he had loved his woman. She wouldn't put it past him. Yet she didn't condemn him for his loyalty to his hometown, or to his own dreams.

He downed his second cup of coffee, glanced at his wristwatch, and scowled. "I've really got to run," he said apologetically as he brought his empty plate to the sink. "I'll pick you up around five-thirty tonight, okay?"

"Okay."

She accompanied him to the living room, where he picked up his jacket, and then to the door. He kissed her gently, then gave her one last perusal. "Are you going to be all right today?" he asked.

"I'll be fine," she promised.

"You've got my number at work if you need me," he reminded her quietly.

She grinned and shoved him out the door, his compassion beginning to overwhelm her. "Get out of here, Nick," she scolded him, though the dancing light in her eyes conveyed how pleased she was by his having taken care of her last night. "Go be a bum at O.R."

Once he was gone, she returned to the kitchen to finish cleaning up. As she stacked the dishes in the dishwasher and then scoured the skillet, she reviewed what Nick had told her about his two "close calls." If she'd come home from a grisly war to discover that her lover had taken up with someone else in her absence, she didn't think she'd want to remain in the same town as the person who'd broken her heart. As it was, she'd chosen to escape from the Long Island town where her heart had been broken by Phil's death.

And if she'd been in love with someone and that person had decided to move to California, Cecily didn't know whether she'd be strong enough not to drop everything and follow her loved one across the continent. She'd never felt such sturdy roots, such an unbreakable attachment to the place where she'd grown up. And the place where she'd grown up was so much nicer than Glenville.

Obviously she was missing something. She doubted she'd ever love Glenville as much as Nick did, but if she loved Nick—and that was fast becoming an irrefutable fact, she admitted—then she wanted to learn to love the city he loved.

Grabbing a sweater and her purse, she left her apartment and hurried downstairs to the parking lot. She climbed into her car and steered to Congdon Street and down, away from the snobbish Heights, to the part of Glenville that belonged to Nick.

She followed the route he'd taken her on last week, cruising past the shops and the City Hall building, missing the street where his parents lived but driving down a residential street nearly identical to it, then navigating west to the train trestle under which Nick had played as a boy. She tried to picture him young, a dark and dashing youth with a sinewy body and a nearly explosive energy. Maybe he'd had only two "close calls" with women, but Cecily couldn't help suspecting that plenty of other women had fallen in love

with Nick Faro over the years. How could they help themselves?

She drove as far as the driveway to O.R., then made a U-
turn. She didn't know whether Nick's office had a window
overlooking the lot and the road, but if it did, she didn't
want him to spot her and think she was spying on him. She
headed back toward town, and after a couple of missed
turns, she found the cul-de-sac where Darlene's Diner was
located.

She parked and entered, pausing in the vestibule to purchase a copy of the local newspaper from a vending machine. Then she took a seat at an empty booth along the wall
and ordered a cup of coffee. If the plump middle-aged
waitress whom Nick had greeted as Alice recognized Cecily, she didn't indicate it.

Sipping her coffee, Cecily turned her attention to the
newspaper. She deliberately avoided reading any of the national or international articles off the wires and instead
concentrated only on the local stories: Glenville's mayor
kicking off a United Way fundraising campaign, a group of
farmers to the north of Glenville joining a national lobby-
ing group in favor of price supports, an item about the increased number of patrons at a neighborhood soup
kitchen—and the increase in contributions to the soup
kitchen. Reading the articles in the grungy back-alley diner
made Cecily feel, if not like a native, then definitely like an
immigrant in Glenville.

After finishing her coffee, she left the diner and drove
back to the center of town. She parked on Main Street and
ambled along the sidewalk, windowshopping. On a whim
she entered Fisher's, the largest department store in the
downtown district. She hadn't bought any new clothing
since Phil died. Today, she decided, it was time to buy
something brand new.

She browsed among the racks, feeling ridiculously extravagant. The sweaters were pretty, but she really didn't need any sweaters. Nor any pants, or dresses. She had all the shoes she needed, all the gloves, the scarves.

Somehow she found herself in the lingerie department. A timid smile played across her lips as she moved past the nightgowns to the "intimate apparel" section. Cecily wasn't the sort to dress up in sensuous, slinky underthings, but maybe now, maybe for tonight...

She spotted a camisole of beige satin and moved to the rack to inspect it. In fact, it was almost more lace than satin—lace cups, a lace hem, lace trim running down the sides. It was truly exquisite. Cecily was struck by how absurdly frivolous it would be to buy such a lovely garment and then hide it beneath one's blouse.

Taking a deep breath, she pulled it from its hanger, checked its size, and plucked a matching pair of satin-and-lace panties from the shelf beneath. Before she could change her mind, she moved swiftly to the cashier's counter and bought the ensemble.

Gathering up her receipt and the bag and strolling through the store to the front door, she stifled a giddy giggle. She'd never worn underwear like this camisole with Phil—but perhaps she should have. He probably would have loved it. Maybe he would have stopped accusing her of being a prude if she'd worn things that sexy.

She *wasn't* a prude. Lingerie might not be the sort of thing one associated with prim, proper schoolteachers, but tonight she wasn't going to be a teacher. She was going to be a woman. *Tonight,* she thought, the husky sonorousness of Nick's voice echoing inside her. *Tonight.* Her impulse to giggle vanished and her heartbeat sped slightly.

Given the erotic thoughts swirling through her brain, she was particularly embarrassed to bump into Annie Munsey

You know the thrill of
escaping to a world of
PASSION...SENSUALITY
...DESIRE...SEDUCTION...
and LOVE FULFILLED...

Escape again...with 4 FREE novels and

get more great Silhouette Desire novels —for a 15-day FREE examination— delivered to your door every month!

Silhouette Desire offers you real-life drama and romance of successful women in charge of their lives and their careers, women who face the challenges of today's world to make their dreams come true. They are not for everyone, they're for women who want a sensual, provocative reading experience.

These are modern love stories that begin where other romances leave off. They take you *beyond* the others and into a world of love fulfilled and passions realized. You'll share precious, private moments and secret dreams...experience every whispered word of love, every ardent touch, every passionate heartbeat. And now you can enter the unforgettable world of Silhouette Desire romances each and every month.

FREE BOOKS

You can start today by taking advantage of this special offer— 4 new Silhouette Desire romances (a $9.00 Value) *absolutely FREE*, along with a Mystery Gift. Just fill out and mail the attached postage-paid order card.

AT-HOME PREVIEWS, FREE DELIVERY

After you receive your 4 free books and Mystery Gift, every month you'll have the chance to preview 6 more Silhouette Desire romances—*as soon as they are published*. When you decide to keep them, you'll pay just $11.70, (a $13.50 Value), *with no additional charges of any kind and no risk!* You can cancel your subscription at any time just by dropping us a note. In any case, the first 4 books and Mystery Gift are yours to keep.

EXTRA BONUS

When you take advantage of this offer, we'll also send you the Silhouette Books Newsletter free with every shipment. Every informative issue features news on upcoming titles, interviews with your favorite authors, and even their favorite recipes.

Get a Free
Mystery Gift, too!

**EVERY BOOK YOU RECEIVE WILL BE
A BRAND-NEW FULL-LENGTH NOVEL!**

CLIP AND MAIL THIS POSTPAID CARD TODAY!

NO POSTAGE
NECESSARY
IF MAILED
IN THE
UNITED STATES

BUSINESS REPLY CARD
FIRST CLASS   PERMIT NO. 194   CLIFTON, N.J.

Postage will be paid by addressee

**Silhouette Books
120 Brighton Road
P.O. Box 5084
Clifton, NJ 07015-9956**

Escape with 4 Silhouette Desire novels (a $9.00 Value) and get a Mystery Gift, too!

Silhouette ❤️ Desire®

Silhouette Books, 120 Brighton Rd., P.O. Box 5084, Clifton, NJ 07015-9956

Yes, please send me FREE and without obligation, 4 new Silhouette Desire novels along with my Mystery Gift. Unless you hear from me after I receive my 4 FREE books, please send me 6 new Silhouette Desire novels for a free 15-day examination each month as soon as they are published. I understand that you will bill me a total of just $11.70 (a $13.50 Value), with no additional charges of any kind. There is no minimum number of books that I must buy, and I can cancel at any time. The first 4 books and Mystery Gift are mine to keep, even if I never take a single additional book.

NAME _____

              (please print)

ADDRESS _____

CITY _____ STATE _____ ZIP _____

Terms and prices subject to change. Your enrollment is subject to acceptance by Silhouette Books.
SILHOUETTE DESIRE and colophon are registered trademarks.

CT7725

just outside Fisher's front door. Her cheeks darkening with color, Cecily clutched her bag and offered silent thanks that it wasn't transparent, displaying her purchase to Nick's sister. "Hello!" she greeted the slender, dark-haired woman.

Annie seemed startled by their collision as well, and she took a moment to recover. "Oh! Hello, Mrs. Adams."

Cecily absorbed the formal salutation. Did Annie want to think of Cecily only as her son's teacher? Well, Cecily might be Bruce's teacher, but she was about to become Nick's lover, and now was probably as good a time as any to establish a less stilted relationship with Annie. "Please call me Cecily," she requested with a genuine smile.

Annie shifted uncomfortably, but her piercing eyes remained unwavering on Cecily's face. "All right," she reluctantly agreed. "Cecily."

They stood awkwardly for a moment, neither speaking. Cecily recalled Annie's whispered comment to Nick last week at the football game, declaring her surprise at her brother's choice in female companionship. She wondered if there was a casual way to prove to Annie that she wasn't an intellectual snob—or, for that matter, the social snob her address might imply. All she could think of to say was, "Has Bruce gotten any word from Ohio State yet?"

"No, not yet," Annie replied. "He told us you said you think he'll do all right in college."

"I certainly do," Cecily said, suffering some dismay that the conversation was veering towards the egghead-ish. "He's got a game today, hasn't he?"

"An away game," Annie said with a nod. "In fact, I really should be on my way, since we've got a bit of a drive to see him play." She took a step towards an aged Chevrolet parked at the curb, then hesitated. "Are you and Nicholas going to the game?"

Cecily was oddly heartened by Annie's remark; it implied that she wasn't averse to thinking of Nick and Cecily as a twosome. "I'm afraid not," she answered. "Nick's got to work today."

"Oh. Right," Annie said, nodding again.

She reached for the doorhandle, and Cecily realized that if she didn't say something quickly she'd miss her chance. "Annie," she said, approaching the woman, who immediately released the handle and turned back to Cecily. "Annie, it isn't going to cause Bruce any problems if I date Nick, is it?"

"No, of course not," Annie hastily replied.

"The kids at school aren't going to rag him about it?"

"Hey, he's a football star," Annie scoffed. "Kids are very careful about ragging some guy who's six-foot-three and weighs as much as Bruce does."

Cecily laughed. "I guess that's true," she concurred, then plowed ahead. "Does it bother you?" she asked bravely.

Annie appeared bewildered. "Why should it?" She smiled bashfully. "Between you and me, I'd rather see Nicholas with someone like you than with some of the dingbats he's dated in his life."

Cecily suspected that Annie rarely praised Nick's girl friends, and she was delighted by the compliment. "I'm a change of pace for him, is that it?" she hazarded.

"Well..." Annie wrestled with her words. "I'll tell you what it is, Cecily. It's that Nicholas always hated school, and he hated everything and everyone that had anything to do with school. So if I seem a little surprised that he's taken up with a teacher, well, it's only that I can't forget what he used to think of teachers."

"Most kids hate school," Cecily observed tolerantly. "A smart teacher doesn't take it personally."

"Yeah. Well, Nicholas isn't in school anymore, and he's not a kid anymore. So it doesn't really matter, does it." She opened her door, and her smile expanded as she climbed in. "See you," she said.

Cecily rehashed her conversation with Annie as she climbed into her own car and headed for home. It wasn't all that surprising to her that as a student Nick hadn't been wild about school, especially when she recalled his reaction to her invitation for him to speak at the school's career assembly next week. He'd remarked that the assemblies had been boring—and maybe they had been, to someone like Nick, who had his own ambitions and enough intelligence to achieve his goals. So many young people despised school on principle; Cecily considered it one of the major challenges of her job to keep her pupils from loathing her. She prided herself on her success in that aspect of her job.

She herself had always adored school—not simply the excitement of learning things, but the actual routines and disciplines of it. While she'd chafed at rules which seemed silly or autocratic to her, she'd enjoyed the daily tasks and pressures. She'd loved the hum of energy in the corridors between classes, the compact designs of the desks, the mar- bled black-and-white cardboard covers of her notebooks. She'd taken pleasure in even the most tedious classes, de- vising secret strategies to keep herself attentive and over- looking the inadequacies of her teachers. She approached her best teachers with a respect bordering on awe. Society might slight teachers, underpay them and overwork them, but Cecily considered them among God's chosen, the lead- ers and role-models who could change a young person's life in all sorts of miraculous ways.

She'd known that her affection for school made her something of an oddball, so she'd always kept her feelings well hidden. She'd complained with her classmates about the homework and the regimentation. She'd joined in their snickering critiques of their teachers. She'd indulged in occasional flings with rule-breaking, sneaking out of a study hall to play cards in the chorus room, or taking three clandestine puffs of a shared cigarette in the second-floor girls' room—and choking for ten minutes afterwards. Those were the rites of passage for an adolescent girl, and she'd performed them without ever revealing her true fondness for school. In fact, she was certain that many of her friends, while cutting study hall and smoking in the lavatory and all the rest of it, harbored the same fondness for school that she felt. But it was taboo to express that fondness, so none of them had ever revealed that they were happy students.

Perhaps Nick had proclaimed his hatred of school, as Cecily had, because it was "cool." Perhaps he'd done it, as she had, so he'd be accepted by his peers. Even if he honestly had hated school, she'd never hold such a sentiment against him. As Annie had said, Nick was no longer a kid. His behavior around Cecily proved that he clearly held some teachers in high esteem.

She'd have to discuss the assembly with him soon. Gary Czymanski had been badgering her all week, and she'd put him off as best she could, promising him that over the weekend she'd talk to the potential speaker she knew. She'd intended to discuss the assembly with Nick last night, but for understandable reasons they'd never gotten around to it. Tonight she'd convince him to participate in the panel. He'd contribute a great deal to the presentation; she knew the students would listen to someone like Nick more readily than to most other speakers. If anyone could persuade them that determination and dedication, education and self-pride paved the road to success in life, Nick could.

Once home, she undressed and showered. Thoughts about the assembly were replaced by thoughts about the evening looming ahead. She felt not an ounce of doubt, not an iota of foreboding about letting Nick love her tonight, about letting their relationship express itself physically. As the shower's spray pounded down on her, she once again heard Phil's voice whispering to her in its liquid hiss: "I like him, Cecily. And more importantly, *you* like him. He's a good man. Take the plunge."

After drying her hair, she pulled her new camisole and panties from the bag and slipped them on. She ought to have tried them on for size in the store. But she'd been strangely bashful about buying such suggestive underwear, and she knew that if she'd given herself a moment's pause by shutting herself inside a fitting booth, she'd have chickened out. Fortunately, they fit her perfectly. She appraised her reflection in the full-length mirror behind her door and realized that they really weren't all that suggestive—more subtle than obvious. Millions of women probably bought far more revealing garments every day of the year.

But…Cecily grinned sheepishly as she observed the shadows of her breasts through the lace, and the seductively skimpy cut of the panties. She felt more exposed in the camisole than she did in an ordinary bra, even though a bra covered much less of her. Something about the way the lace tantalized the eye with glimpses of what was lurking underneath it, something about the smooth sheen of the satin, made Cecily feel a bit self-conscious. Maybe she did have a touch of the prude in her.

She felt the urge to chicken out again, but continued dressing nevertheless, donning a cream-colored cashmere sweater and gray wool slacks. As long as she couldn't see her new undergarments she could forget she was wearing them.

At five-thirty, Nick arrived. He'd replaced his slept-in suit with a flannel shirt featuring a plaid of pale and dark blue, and a pair of new jeans. He'd shaved, too, and he appeared far more alert than he'd looked that morning. Cecily wondered remorsefully how uncomfortable he must have been on the couch, how much more comfortable he would have been in her bed...No. Last night would have been wrong. And if Nick climbed onto the bed with her, even if he too had remained on top of the blanket and fully clothed, neither of them would have gotten much rest at all.

Tonight would be different, and an unspoken awareness of that fact hovered in the air between them as they greeted each other. Nick's brief kiss on Cecily's cheek was restrained, but anticipation glowed in his eyes and warmed his tentative smile. "All set?" he asked.

Cecily understood that his question connoted far more than its obvious meaning. But she replied, "I'll just get my bag, and then we'll go."

They descended to the ground floor and climbed into Nick's Porsche. "Are we going someplace snobby tonight?" she asked as he steered out of the complex.

"Absolutely not," he asserted, turning right and coasting down the hill.

They drove in silence through downtown to the neighborhood south of it, passing several blocks of small, narrow houses. When Nick signaled left and veered onto a driveway beside a compact brick house that resembled all the other houses on the street, Cecily realized that he'd taken her to his home. Again her pulse sped slightly, but her voice emerged evenly when she asked, "Am I going to be treated to your culinary talents tonight?"

"My talents, yes," Nick responded. Cecily was once more aware of the implications that colored his most offhanded remarks.

He parked his car in the garage shed at the end of the driveway, and they walked down the paved strip past a vest-pocket backyard and the side of the house in order to enter through the front door. Nick's porch was in better condition than the one at his parents' house, its planks level and freshly painted. He unlocked the door and ushered Cecily into a front hall, which opened onto a square living room.

The living room was small but homey. Nick switched on a torch lamp beside the overstuffed couch so Cecily could admire the room. The walls were white, the hardwood floor buffed to a high gloss, the area rug a bright orange. Two brown overstuffed easy chairs matched the sofa, and the outer wall contained a fireplace of natural brick. "It's lovely," Cecily exclaimed, delighted by the comfortable atmosphere of the modest room.

"You don't think it's past its heyday?" he teased as he led her toward the old-fashioned kitchen, by way of a rectangular dining room, its table already set with two places and an unlit candle centerpiece.

"I think you've done wonders with it," Cecily said, studying the cheerful yellow ceramic tiles decorating the wall above the gas stove. "I can't feel the shadow of the smokestack here at all."

"Of course you can't. It's practically dark out," Nick joked. "Smokestack shadows have a funny way of disappearing at night." He moved to the stove and lifted the lids of two large pots on it. Setting the lids back in place, he lit the burners under each. Then he pulled a plastic bag of spaghetti from a cabinet and untwisted the tie holding it shut.

Cecily crossed the brightly lit room and studied the bag of pasta. "Did you make this yourself?" she asked.

He grinned and shook his head. "My mother did," he told her. "She makes the stuff in bulk and farms it out to her bachelor son. Mama Faro's first commandment is, 'Thou shalt not eat spaghetti that comes out of a box.'"

"After eating this, I'll be so spoiled I won't want to eat spaghetti out of a box anymore," Cecily said with a sigh. She lifted the lid of the smaller pot and peeked inside. It was filled with a rich sauce, chunks of tomatoes and mushrooms thickening it. As it heated up, its spicy aroma intensified. "Did Mama Faro make this too?" Cecily asked.

"No, I take full credit for that," Nick boasted.

"It smells delicious," she noted, lowering the lid. "When did you have time to make sauce? I thought you were working today."

"I made a batch last week and froze it," Nick explained. "Commandment Number Two in the Faro family is, 'Always cook in bulk.'"

The water in the larger pot began to boil, and Nick tossed some spaghetti into it. "Is there anything I can do to help? Cecily offered.

"You could slice and butter the bread," Nick said, gesturing toward a long loaf of Italian bread on the counter. He pulled a knife from a drawer for her, and plucked a tub of butter from a shelf of his refrigerator.

"This is beginning to look like a pretty fattening meal," Cecily said cheerfully as she sliced the bread.

"Oh—thanks for reminding me," said Nick, swinging open the refrigerator door again and sliding out a large bowl of salad. "Here, skin-and-bones," he announced, displaying the bowl for her before carrying it to the dining room. "That's supposed to make up for all the starch."

He returned to the kitchen and stooped down in front of another cabinet, searching for a bottle of wine. He pulled out a straw-wrapped jug of Chianti and applied a corkscrew to its top. Cecily set down the butter knife and turned to watch him uncork the bottle. She studied the line of concentration marking his brow, and the flexing of his shoulders as he wrestled with the cork. Her gaze traveled down his lean body and she smiled. "Talk about skin and bones," she sniffed. "I bet you don't eat like this every night."

He eyed her and laughed. "You're going to hate me for saying this," he warned her, "but I happen to have something in common with your late husband—I can eat everything in sight and never gain a pound."

"I hate you," Cecily breezily confirmed. Nick laughed again. "What's your sport?" she asked.

"Hmm?"

"You're built like an athlete," she observed. "Not a football player, though. I'd guess basketball."

"Baseball," he corrected her.

She ran her eyes back up his body, measuring his towering height. "You're too tall for baseball," she objected.

"So's Dave Winfield. Actually, height does have its advantage in baseball, even if it gives you a huge strike zone. I can catch some pretty high fly balls." He poured the wine into two goblets and passed one to her, then stirred his pasta. "Nowadays I play softball. O.R. has a great team. Last year we beat all three teams from Glenville Industries."

"You're the captain?"

"No way!" he chuckled. "I spend enough of my life leading the guys. When it comes to playing, I let someone else take the reins."

Their meal was ready, and they retired with their wine to the dining room. Nick lit the candle before sitting opposite Cecily at the oval table. He watched attentively as she tasted the spaghetti and sauce. "Mmm," she murmured contentedly. "Definitely worth gaining weight over."

His gentle smile indicated his pleasure. Cecily took her turn watching him eat for a moment. The candle's flame cast a flickering golden light across his features, and her breath caught in her throat as she considered how attractive he was, how strikingly virile. Her imagination drifted to what would occur after dinner, and she briskly forced her attention back to the meal. "I bumped into your sister to-day," she remarked. "Literally."

"Oh? Where?"

"Downtown."

"What were you doing downtown?" Nick asked.

"Shopping," Cecily said, and the reminder of what she'd bought caused her thoughts to veer to after-dinner notions again. She took a deep breath to compose herself. "Annie and I had a nice chat," she continued. "She told me you used to hate school."

Nick rolled his eyes. "Leave it to her to blab something like that," he muttered with annoyance. "Once a tattle-tale, always a tattle-tale."

"Did you hate school?" Cecily pressed him.

He ruminated for a moment, then nodded. "Afraid so."

"Why?"

"Because I didn't have any teachers as pretty as you," he teased. Cecily's refusal to smile caused him to grow seri-ous. "I'm not too happy when it comes to authority fig-ures," he explained slowly. "It wasn't school I hated so much as having all those people telling me what to do all the time."

"I'd think the army would be worse than school."

"It was," Nick granted. "God, I hated that part of it. Well, I hated the whole thing of it, but...I'm just not too good at taking orders."

"Still, you managed to get yourself an education," Ce-cily commented.

"There are plenty of ways to get an education if you want one," Nick remarked cryptically. "But you're right, I got one. Annie," he grunted, shaking his head. "Big sisters can be a pain."

"You could have done worse," Cecily defended Annie. She recalled what Annie had said about the "dingbats" Nick had dated in the past, and wondered whether he and his sister often argued about his relationships with women. "I suppose if you want to stay in your hometown you have to put up with some occasional interference from your family."

"It comes with the territory," Nick agreed before taking a long drink of wine. "Are you glad to be away from yours?"

Cecily nodded. "I love my parents," she admitted honestly. "But after Phil's death they interfered to such an extent that I thought I'd go insane. I don't blame them—I know they had the best of intentions. But I just couldn't remain so close to them. I had to get away."

"So you escape the interference, and also the home-made spaghetti."

Cecily perused him thoughtfully. She understood what he was saying—that there was a positive side to his situation, that despite interference from his relatives he was glad to live near them. "My parents don't make home-made spaghetti," Cecily declared. "My mother's first commandment is, 'If it doesn't come pre-mixed, frozen, or in your grocer's dairy case, why bother?'" Nick laughed.

During the remainder of the meal, Nick asked Cecily more about her parents and her childhood. As she described her youth, it sounded dull to her, dull and spoiled. Growing up in the shadow of a smokestack seemed almost exotic compared to the staid upper-middle-class life she'd lived. Although Nick's question conveyed no condemnation of her life, but rather curiosity and even envy, she couldn't muster the sort of pride in her past that he had in his. Her life had been, quite simply, an average suburban existence spent in an elegantly furnished house surrounded by a neatly mowed emerald lawn, in a school where books and supplies were plentiful and college acceptances taken for granted. It was a world in which authority figures were never questioned because they always provided for every need and whim.

As she spoke, she reflected on the thoughts she'd indulged in that morning, when she'd wondered whether she would have been as strong as Nick had been in sticking to his own dreams rather than following his lover's. His background had given him the strength to define himself, to determine his own fate. Until Phil's death, Cecily had never been tested as Nick had been. Only by surviving the tragedy of her young widowhood—not simply surviving it but emerging triumphant over it—had Cecily discovered the wells of strength within herself. She was still in a contemplative mood when they finished their meal and teamed up at the sink to wash the dishes. She pushed her sweater's sleeves up to her elbows, and Nick rolled up his shirtsleeves. She watched him scrub each plate before handing it to her to dry and found herself mesmerized by the strength that emanated from him. The firm hold of his tapered fingers on the slippery dishes, the thick tendons and bones of his wrists, the muscles of his forearms all bespoke a strength that dazzled her.

She thought of that strength as he worked and again as he closed the last cabinet and wiped his hands dry on a towel. Then she lifted her face to his and comprehended the strength in his angular jaw, in his high brow, in the constant darkness of his eyes. She read strength, hope, promise in his gaze.

He took her hand and led her to the stairway leading up from the front hall. Her fingers tensed slightly within his as they started to climb, and he glanced down at her and paused. "Cecily," he whispered.

She lowered her eyes, startled by her unexpected nervousness.

He bowed to kiss the top of her head. "We don't have to, you know," he said softly.

His abounding sensitivity reassured her. He was strong, and so was she, especially now, especially with him. She lifted her face to his and smiled. "I believe you promised me the private tour," she murmured.

"When you're ready."

"I'm ready," she swore.

He kissed her again, then escorted her up the stairs.

Six

He entered his bedroom ahead of Cecily, crossing to the bed and switching on the lamp on his night table. She stepped into the room and surveyed it. It was exactly as she'd envisioned it, a square, compact room with comfortable-looking furniture: a double bed with a brass headboard, a sturdy oak chest of drawers, a plump easy chair, a plush area rug covering the varnished hardwood floor. She smiled.

Nick gathered her into his arms and kissed her profoundly. "I feel like I've been waiting for this forever," he murmured, his fingers digging into the glistening waves of her hair.

"You haven't known me forever," Cecily pointed out.

"No, but I've been waiting all my life for someone like you," he argued. "And now you're here."

He kissed her again, and she curled her arms around him. His hands wandered down her back, gliding across the soft fabric of her sweater to its ribbed edge and lifting it. She drew back so he could remove the sweater. His eyes widened with surprise at the discovery of the delicate camisole underneath. He touched its ribbon-thin shoulder straps, then traced the lace trim down her front to her waist. "I like this," he commented. "I wouldn't have imagined you wearing this sort of thing."

Cecily's cheeks flushed pink. "I don't usually," she admitted. "It's new. I bought it today."

Nick clearly inferred that she'd bought it today for him— which was exactly what she wanted him to know. His smile deepened as he took a step backward and gave the camisole a careful inspection. Mirroring his smile, Cecily reached for the buttons of his shirt and unfastened them, tugging the shirttails from the waistband of his jeans.

His chest was a smooth bronze expanse of rippling skin tapering down to his slim, firm stomach. As Nick's eyes absorbed her, so hers absorbed him. Phil's chest had been covered with hair, and Cecily had never before considered what his hair might have hidden from view. She admired the visible contours of Nick's ribs and muscles, the arching indentations marking the lower edge of his abdomen, the dark, taut circles of his nipples. Merely looking at his torso made her breath grow short with excitement.

Still examining her camisole, he drifted behind her and ran his palms over the sleek satin underlining her shoulder blades. His hands slid beneath her arms, drawing her against him, and he cupped his fingers over her breasts and massaged them. Leaning back into him, she sighed.

His mouth moved through her hair, his warm breath filtering down to the nape of her neck. "You're beautiful," he whispered.

"So are you," she returned, even though all she could see of him was his graceful hands as they caressed her.

"Me? Beautiful?"

"Absolutely," Cecily asserted. "And don't get macho on me and make some ridiculous statement about how men can't be beautiful. You are."

He laughed and moved his fingers to the fly of her slacks. He deftly opened the fastening and let them fall to her ankles. "It's a whole outfit, huh," he observed, exploring the trim of her matching panties with his thumbs.

She shuddered, her thighs tensing as his fingers brushed lightly over them. All she could think of was that she wanted him to remove the outfit he was so taken with. But he only continued to tease her, running his fingers along the elastic edge of the panties, then inching his hands beneath the camisole to touch her belly.

Frustrated by his leisurely pace, she turned to face him and tugged his shirt from his shoulders. He obediently lifted his hands from her to shed the shirt, then guided her to the belt of his jeans. By the time she had it unbuckled, he was sliding off the panties and then the camisole. He stepped out of his jeans and led her to the bed, dropping onto it beside her.

He urged her body snugly against his and kissed her again. His legs moved along and between hers, and his hands traveled over the rest of her, stroking her throat, her shoulders, her arms and sides. His lips roved across her face, pausing to browse at her temples, at the hinge of her jaw, the dainty point of her chin.

Cecily in turn set her hands free to learn his body. His build was different from Phil's, leaner, longer, his hairless chest a mystery of sinuous movement under her probing fingertips, his hips hard and narrow, flexing at her timid touch.

One of his hands closed over her breast, shaping to its soft roundness, pressing gently into the throbbing red bud at its peak. She moaned softly, arching toward him, shifting slightly to increase the contact between their bodies. Her hips arched to him as well, savoring his arousal, delighting in the rough groan that tore itself from his lungs.

Almost reluctantly, his hand abandoned her breast and moved down her body, playing across the sharp angle of her hipbone before reaching between her legs. The fluid heat that welled up within her stunned her. She closed her eyes, succumbing to the dazzling return of sensations that had been lying undisturbed inside her for so long. The wait had been worth it, she knew. She would have trusted no one but Nick to awaken them, to rediscover them, to give her back everything that was lost two long years ago.

Her body moved with his hand and her fingers gripped his shoulders, clinging to him as her flesh tingled in the blazing return of feeling. Sensing her readiness, he rose fully onto her and drove deep into her.

His thrusts were slow, controlled, almost languid. His rhythm was completely different from Phil's.... Cecily quickly chastised herself for allowing thoughts of Phil to intrude at that moment. All she wanted to think of was Nick, loving him, receiving his love.

She felt another flood of warmth rush through her, sweet and intoxicating. It wasn't building, simply flowing, surging, bathing every cell and nerve in her body. She realized that she couldn't expect more, and she didn't mind. It felt marvelous simply to be so close to Nick, to share herself with him. It felt marvelous to take his masculine strength into her, to surround him with her own feminine softness, to be his woman, to have her man.

Her arms tightened around him and his tempo increased. She felt the elastic strain in the muscles of his back, the tension in his hips, the suddenly unbridled power of his thrusts as he careened toward a crest. He stopped breathing for an instant, then surrendered to his body's release, groaning Cecily's name.

He sank down onto her and she hugged him protectively. She felt his lips moving slowly against her shoulder and then her ear as he buried his face in the crook of her neck. His body grew still. He said nothing.

"Nick," she whispered.

Hesitantly he raised his head. His eyes beat down on her, darkened by troubling shadows. "Cecily," he began haltingly, then looked away. "This wasn't..." His voice drifted off.

She lifted her hand to his cheek and eased his face back to hers. "It was wonderful, Nick. Don't apologize."

"Wonderful?" He scowled in disbelief.

"You were the one who said the first time's always rough going," she reminded him with a tender smile.

He slid off her, dropping onto the mattress and tucking one arm beneath her to hold her close. "So it was rough going," he confirmed grimly.

"No," she hastily corrected herself. "No, Nick, it was wonderful."

"I wanted..." He gazed earnestly at her. "I wanted it to be perfect for you."

"There's no such thing as perfection," she disputed him gently.

He remained solemn. "I used to think that myself," he agreed. "And then I met you."

"Me?" She was unable to suppress an amazed laugh. "I'm not perfect, Nick."

"You're not?" He appeared about to argue, then permitted himself a tenuous smile. "My idea of perfection is a gorgeous woman with hair like yours, all that red mixed in with the brown...and eyes so big and bright...and this gorgeous woman races across the schoolyard and flings her arms around me and calls me 'sweetheart.' That's perfection.''

"Maybe calling you 'sweetheart' was perfection," Cecily allowed with a chuckle. "But I assure you, I'm not perfect."

"What's not perfect about you?" he challenged her.

She laughed again as she considered the question. "I blush too easily," she remarked.

"You look perfect when you blush," he refuted her.

"I'm obsessively neat. I'm compulsive about getting things done on time—like wanting to grade papers the day they're turned in. You've seen that yourself."

"So you're disciplined," he said, turning her self-criticism into a compliment.

"I hate people like you, who can eat everything and never gain weight," she tried.

He shook his head, rejecting her attempt. "That sounds like a perfectly reasonable reaction," he said.

She lapsed into silent thought, and her smile didn't return when she murmured, "Nick, if I were perfect, I would have responded perfectly just now. We wouldn't even be having this discussion."

He considered her statement, then pulled her closer to himself, cushioning her head with his shoulder. "Was it—" He swallowed, then forced out the words. "Was it always good with him?"

His question astonished her, and she took a moment to recover. Was Nick jealous of Phil? Competing with him? Had he been able to discern that her mind had wandered, however briefly, to Phil during their lovemaking?

It didn't matter. Nick was being honest with her, brutally honest, exposing his own insecurities. She accepted his question in that light, and answered it as best she could. "No, of course not," she began, then thought some more and reversed herself. "Yes," she said, edging back so she could see him. "If you're asking me whether there were fireworks every time we made love, no, Nick, there weren't. Sometimes there were fireworks and sometimes just warmth and comfort. But when you love someone, really love him...Yes, it's always good."

He measured her with his piercing eyes. "And it was good now?" he asked hesitantly.

"Yes," she vowed, her voice quiet but firm.

He was able to deduce what she was telling him. She loved him, really loved him. That was what counted; that was what made sex good.

He leaned forward to kiss her, a loving kiss that bound them together as forcefully as their physical coupling and their heartfelt confessions. His hands roamed down her spine to her waist, and he rolled her onto her back again. Hovering above her, he gazed down at her. "I still want to satisfy you," he insisted in a husky voice.

"I'm satisfied."

He shook his head. "Tell me," he implored her, letting his fingers journey across her stomach, up between her breasts to her collarbone and along its slender ridge. "Tell me how he satisfied you."

"Nick." She laughed. "We were married five and a half years, for heaven's sake. It takes time to learn about each other, to learn what pleases your lover."

"I don't want to wait five and a half years," He covered her lips with his, penetrated them with his tongue, conquered the trembling recesses of her mouth. "Does kissing please you?" he asked hoarsely once he'd ended the kiss.

"Yes."

"Here?" he asked, shifting on the bed and touching his mouth to her breast.

"Yes."

She sighed as his tongue swirled over the swollen nipple. He sucked on it for several moments, then moved his lips to her other breast. "Here?"

"Yes," she mouthed, her voice growing weak as another, fresher surge of heat washed through her. His teeth tenderly scraped the rosy tip and she sighed again, feeling the heat flare and burn its way down from her chest to her hips.

He shifted again, grazing her navel with his lips. "Here?"

She nodded, unable to speak. The blaze built within her, astounding her with its unexpected intensity. His mouth moved lower, and when he gently spread her legs apart with his hands, she almost cried out in shock. She had never been kissed this way before, and the wild grip of sensation that seized her was almost unbearably excruciating. Earlier her flesh had been nudged awake, but now it was being jolted, shaken, ravaged.

She reached for Nick, her hands fisting in his hair as he compelled her body to the response he wanted, the fiery womanly response that had earlier eluded them both. She was powerless to resist it, powerless before Nick's determination to reach his own satisfaction by satisfying her. She was powerless to do anything but respond, concede, surrender.

Her soul tensed, then exploded, shooting pulsing flames throughout her body, fierce spasms of ecstasy that burned away everything but her love for him. A choked sob escaped her, and her hands slowly unfurled, moving dazedly through the dense black silk of his hair. His head came to rest wearily against her abdomen, and she continued to comb her fingers through his hair and down to his shoulders, taking relief in the solid shape of him.

Finally he drew himself up to lie beside Cecily. She cuddled close to him, and he enveloped her in his arms. They fell asleep that way, their arms and lips and bodies expressing all that needed to be said.

"I like waking up to you," Nick declared as he plugged in his percolator. "This could become habit-forming."

Cecily leaned back in her chair. She was clad in her panties and an oversized shirt of Nick's, but her bare legs were warmed by the morning sun pouring through the kitchen window beside her. "Maybe you ought to be careful so you won't become addicted," she affectionately warned him.

"It's probably too late," he said, pretending dismay. "I'm already hooked." He carried a box of cornflakes and a bottle of milk to the tiny table, then set it with bowls and spoons. Cecily was glad that he didn't prepare a more substantial breakfast. After the previous night's filling dinner, she didn't have much appetite.

"Addicted, huh," she mocked him as he poured the coffee and then took his seat opposite her. "Sounds serious."

He angled his head to study her long, exposed legs. "If you don't want me to go through the agonies of withdrawal, you'd better stick around," he demanded. "Those legs don't look flimsy to me at all. What's *your* sport?"

"I'm a first-class klutz," Cecily lamented. "I don't have a sport at all."

"Sure you do," he said, his eyes glinting wickedly. "I saw you in action last night." He swallowed a spoonful of cereal and chuckled. "You know what I'd like to do?" he commented. "I'd like to show up at the school tomorrow and announce on the P.A. system what Mrs. Adams and I discussed over breakfast."

"Try it," she muttered, brandishing a threatening fist. "You'll be minced meat by lunchtime."

"And then they'll serve me in the cafeteria," he supposed. "Is the food still so godawful at Glenville High?"

"Wretched," she confirmed. "An excellent incentive for those of us who can't eat everything in sight without gaining a ton." She sipped her juice and considered the subject of Glenville High. "Nick, will you speak at the assembly next Friday?"

"What assembly?"

"The career assembly." At his confused scowl, she reminded him, "I told you about it on the phone when you were in St. Louis."

"Oh, that," he remembered with a snort.

His disdain for the assembly disappointed her. "I know you said those assemblies used to be boring when you were a pupil, Nick, but I think you'd make a wonderful speaker. Won't you at least consider it?"

"How'd you get stuck lining up the speakers?" he asked, avoiding addressing her remark directly. "Is that the sort of chore they lay on the newcomers?"

"No. One of my colleagues is in charge of it. He arranged for two speakers, but the third one backed out on him. He asked if I knew anyone, and I immediately thought of you."

"Of course you thought of me," Nick chided her. "You don't know too many other people in town."

"That's not why I thought of you," Cecily maintained. "I thought of you because you'd have a lot to contribute to the assembly."

He frowned and shook his head. "I don't think so, Cecily. There are other people better at that kind of thing than I am."

"But—" She scrambled for an argument. She didn't stop to ponder why it meant so much to her that Nick participate in the assembly. All she knew was that he belonged there. "You say you love Glenville so much."

"I do," he confirmed.

"Then why won't you do this for the kids of Glenville?"

He rolled his eyes. "I do plenty for the kids of Glenville," he claimed. "I've donated money to fix up a playground, and last spring I hit up a bunch of folks for money to buy new uniforms and equipment for the high school's baseball team. Maybe I haven't organized any hospital runs, but I do what I can. I'm not good at standing up in front of a pack of students and saying, 'Follow my example.' That's just not my style."

His comment about hospital runs made Cecily wonder once again whether Nick felt at all competitive toward her former husband. But she decided to let the subject drop for now. He seemed unrelenting in his resistance to speaking at the assembly.

His smile returned as he swallowed the last of his coffee. "Do you have any papers to grade compulsively today?" he asked.

She shook her head.

"Good. There's something I want to show you, if you're interested."

"Oh?" She eyed him inquisitively. "What?"

"It's a surprise," he said with an enigmatic grin. Standing, he gathered the dishes and brought them to the sink.

Cecily helped him wash them, then watched with building curiosity as he slapped together several cheese sandwiches and wrapped them in foil. "Are we going on a picnic?" she asked.

"Something like that," he said mysteriously. "Go put on your clothes and we'll head off. Unless, of course, you'd rather stay dressed like this," he added, reaching beneath the shirt to goose her.

She slapped his hand away. "Forget it," she scolded with feigned disgust. "Keep your addiction in check, Mr. Faro."

"You're asking the impossible!" he shouted after her in protest as she fled up the stairs.

Once she was dressed, they left his house through the kitchen door and crossed the back yard to the garage. Cecily smiled privately as she contemplated her visit to his house. Last night he'd wanted her to enter it properly, through the front door, but she preferred using the back door. It seemed the more natural exit, and she felt at home using it.

Once they were settled in the car, Nick steered up the hill to the Heights. "We're going someplace snobby?" Cecily guessed mischievously as they cruised past the grand houses lining the boulevard.

"Uh-uh."

"Where?" she asked.

"Be patient," he reproached her.

"That's another of my shortcomings," she informed him. "I'm not very patient. Where in the world did you get the idea that I was perfect?"

"By looking at you," he answered simply. "Maybe you're the classic case of looks being deceiving." His wink informed her that he was teasing.

They drove beyond the outskirts of the city, following a route that cut through farm acreage. Some of the fields were still lush with greenery, but most had already been harvested. In the distance, Cecily spotted a farmer riding a tractor and turning his soil. "It's hard to believe such bucolic scenery can exist so close to an industrial city like Glenville," she mused.

"Are there farms on Long Island?" Nick asked.

She shrugged. "A few, out in the eastern portion of the island. Potato farms, mostly. But they keep shrinking as development encroaches. A typical instance of urban sprawl."

"And you think that place is so great," he sniffed contemptuously. "Here we've got everything you'd want—the city and the country, side by side."

She cut herself off before noting that the city in question was rather too ugly to qualify as everything she'd want. The ugliness of Glenville was beginning to strike her as oddly charming. And to exist so near such rolling verdant stretches of farmland enhanced Glenville in her eyes. "Did you used to escape to the country when you were a boy?" she asked.

He cast her a speculative glance. "Good guess," he praised her.

"Oh?"

"Not about what I did as a boy but what I do now." He reached for her hand and squeezed it, stifling the question on her lips. "Be patient. You'll see."

They had driven for nearly an hour when the farmland was overtaken by forest. The road began to twist, arching over hills which, while not steep, were evidently too rugged to plant with crops. The dense trees extending on either side of the road had begun to shed their leaves, but here and there a specimen of blazing autumn foliage still stood, its flaming leaves illuminating the woods.

After another half hour, Nick navigated onto a narrow lane of crushed asphalt which led to a small, pristine lake. The road encircled the lake. He followed it a short distance past several rustic houses until he coasted to a halt on a dirt driveway leading to a porch-lined cabin constructed of split logs. "Surprise," Nick announced as he killed the engine.

Cecily's eyes shimmered with delight as she swung open her door. "Is this yours?"

"This is mine," he said, gathering the bag of sandwiches and accompanying her onto the porch, which overlooked the lake.

"Oh, Nick—it's fantastic!" she crooned ecstatically.

"You'd better reserve judgment until you've seen the inside," he cautioned her as he heaved the screen door open on its rusted hinges and unlocked the inner door.

They stepped into the cabin. It consisted of a single cramped room with unfinished wooden walls and a worn braided rug on its floor. A cot stood against one wall, a chair leaking its upholstery was set between two windows, and a kitchen area including a miniature refrigerator, basin sink, and two-burner stove occupied the far corner. A fishing pole and two rowboat oars were balanced against the wall behind the door. The air held the fresh scent of pine.

"It's fantastic," Cecily repeated as she wandered through the cozy room. She turned back to Nick, who was leaning against the doorframe and gauging her reaction. "How long have you owned it?"

"A couple of years."

She grinned as she approached him. "And here I thought you were Glenville's biggest civic booster," she remonstrated.

"I am," he insisted indignantly. "That doesn't mean I can't keep a little hideaway for myself outside the city limits."

"Then you admit that sometimes you've got to escape from Glenville?"

"Everyone's got to escape sometimes," he maintained, moving to her and folding his arms around her. "I'm glad you like it. I've never brought a woman here before."

His admission thrilled Cecily. But rather than making a big issue of it, she joked, "Sometimes you've got to escape from women, is that what you're saying?"

"Sometimes...sometimes I used to want to escape from women," he whispered, touching her brow with his lips. "Not anymore."

He released her and strode to the refrigerator. When he opened it, Cecily wasn't terribly surprised to find it stocked with several sixpacks of beer and nothing else. He pulled two bottles from a shelf and twisted off their caps. "Picnic?" he suggested.

She nodded enthusiastically. "How about on the porch?"

"How about by the lake?" he overrode her, lugging the bottles and the sandwiches to the door.

They ambled down the dirt driveway to a pebbly stretch of shoreline and sat. While Nick unwrapped the sandwiches, Cecily gazed out at the lake. Its crystalline surface was nearly motionless, reflecting the clear blue sky above it and catching the sun's rays in a blinding strip of light. Two men sat in a rowboat close to the opposite shore, their fishing poles protruding at angles as they enjoyed their own beers in the midday warmth.

"Do you come here often?" Cecily asked, accepting the sandwich Nick offered.

"Not often enough," he said before taking a swig of his beer. "My folks were horrified when I bought this place."

She cast him a surprised look. "Why? Because it's so far from Glenville?"

"Because they thought it was extravagant. Not that it cost me all that much—the cabin isn't Buckingham Palace," he mocked. He consumed his sandwich, immersed in thought. "They still haven't gotten used to the fact that their son can actually have money," he explained. "My mother is constantly nagging me that I should sell the Porsche and buy something sensible, a Dodge pick-up or something. I think…" He lapsed into thought again. "Sometimes I think they believe I've overstepped rank."

"But they must be proud of all you've achieved," Cecily noted.

He nodded. "They're proud, sure. But maybe they think I don't quite deserve it."

"But you do," she argued, her thoughts wandering back to the school assembly. "It seems to me that you've fought for everything you've got, and you've earned it. Without any advantages, without any help. That's why I want you to speak at the school on Friday, Nick. You're such a fine role-model for the students."

"Me?" he scoffed.

His reticence took her aback. Where was the self-pride she'd seen so often in him? Where was his boundless confidence, his boastful arrogance? Did he perhaps agree with his parents that he didn't quite deserve everything he'd attained? "Of course, *you*," she asserted stubbornly: "Nick, what you've achieved is remarkable."

"Hmm," he grunted in consent. "Okay, it's remarkable. But so what?"

"So what?" she erupted. "Glenville High School is filled with young people who think they've got nothing to aspire to, nothing to hope for but a life on the assembly line at Glenville Industries. Someone like you could stand before them and encourage them to aspire to more."

He fingered the label on his beer bottle reflectively. "What other speakers are going to be there?"

"Gary told me he's invited a dentist and a computer specialist at Glenville Central Bank. They'll describe their jobs to the kids, and you'll talk about industrial careers."

"Industrial careers," he grunted. "Sounds like working on an assembly line at Glenville Industries to me."

"It sounds like founding their own companies and making something of themselves. Being able to buy new uniforms for the school teams—or to buy Porsches, if that's what turns them on. Why don't you want to speak, Nick?"

He stared out at the lake, ruminating. "A dentist and a banker, huh," he grumbled, then turned fully to Cecily. "Don't you see? They're nice, cultured professional types."

"Exactly. The students won't identify with them as easily as they would with you."

"I don't want them identifying with me," he muttered. At Cecily's confused look he struggled to explain. "Cecily, I'm not—I'm not such a good role-model for those kids. I've had some pretty rough times in my past. The life I've lived worked out okay for me, but it's not the sort of life kids should be imitating."

"Of course you had rough times," she conceded. "Starting a new business must have been difficult. And Vietnam…God willing, the kids in school today won't have to contend with anything like that. But you're belittling yourself if you think you haven't got something to offer them."

"I'm being honest about myself," he disputed her, turning away again and focusing his vision on the lake. "I'm not like you, I'm not like your husband, I'm not like dentists and bankers. I'm a poor boy who made good the hard way, but my way isn't for most people. We're very different in a lot of ways, Cecily. I'm not like you, don't you see? I'm not like your husband."

He seemed to be wrestling with his thoughts, attempting to convey something that Cecily couldn't fathom. "We're different in the externals," she granted. "We grew up differently, Nick. But our values and ideals are the same. We believe in hard work, discipline, education…"

"Education." He exhaled. "You believe education comes out of books, out of lectures, off of blackboards. I believe it comes out of living, listening to your heart, following your own drummer and all that."

She measured his words. "And you don't think that's a worthwhile lesson to teach today's kids?"

He twisted to her, the severe lines of his face revealing the difficulty he was having expressing himself. "Look. You're a teacher. You went to college, right?"

"College and graduate school," she replied.

"Graduate school, too, huh?"

"I have a master's degree in education. It's required for getting a teacher's license," she told him.

"A master's degree," he murmured. "I didn't go at all."

"To graduate school?"

"To college."

She took a moment to collect her thoughts. She'd just assumed that Nick had gotten a complete education. How could he have accomplished all he had without a degree? In the world she came from, *everyone* went to college. Nobody even questioned that that was what they'd do. It was taken for granted.

Obviously Nick was acutely aware of her attitude, and he feared her condemnation for his having not obtained the sort of education she prized. She couldn't show her disapproval of him; he seemed so vulnerable. "I'm impressed that you've achieved so much without formal training," she said carefully.

"I'm not an idiot," he stated. "I imported Jim to be my partner because he had the book-learning. I figured that had to count for something, and since I didn't have it, I brought him into the picture."

"That shows some intelligence," Cecily allowed, then cringed at her patronizing tone. "Nick, I don't care that you didn't go to college. In your case...that kind of schooling obviously wasn't necessary."

"And you want me to get up before a crowd of students and tell them they can do it without schooling too?"

At last she understood his reluctance to speak to the assembly. He knew that even though he himself had made it without college, Cecily and her fellow teachers might not want their charges to pick up on the sort of message Nick's success would illustrate to them. She also understood his lukewarm comments the day they'd met, when she'd babbled about his nephew's prospects for attending college. Nick had said then that he believed college wasn't for everyone, but that each individual had to decide what was best for himself. Yet he also apparently believed that, given her own enduring love of school and formal education, Cecily might not like an approach such as his. At the very least, she wouldn't want him preaching it to impressionable students at the high school.

But his confession of his lack of education went beyond the matter of the assembly. Nick was evidently fearful of her passing judgment on him. What had he said? *I'm not like you, or like your husband.* He wasn't competing with Phil, but he was comparing himself to Phil, to the teacher who had married the teacher, and he was clearly afraid of not measuring up.

"I don't care whether you went to college," Cecily declared. She was surprised to hear herself say such a thing, but as soon as she voiced the words she knew they were the truth. She was no longer the pampered girl who evaluated everyone based on the number of years they spent in school. She was no longer the schoolmarm, surrounded by like-minded people, never questioning that there could be another path through life. Nick had altered her perspective on Glenville, a place that would have seemed an alien universe to her two years ago. Now he was altering her perspective on education itself. "I want you to speak at the assembly," she whispered.

He cupped his hand over her shoulder and turned her fully to him. "Do you really?"

"Really," she swore.

"You don't mind?"

She knew he was asking her more than whether she minded his lack of a college diploma. "I love you, Nick," she breathed. "Whatever made you what you are, I love you."

He stared at her for a long moment, searching her face. At last he smiled, a shy, curiously grateful smile. He stood, then extended his hand to her and hoisted her to her feet. After gathering their trash, they walked in silence back to the cabin.

Seven

Thanks to the sheltering trees blocking the sun from the roof, the cabin's interior was cool. Cecily and Nick undressed quickly and wordlessly, then huddled on the narrow cot, seeking warmth from each other rather than from the thin woolen blanket folded at the foot of the mattress.

Nick's long arms wrapped around Cecily, drawing her tightly to him. She twisted her fingers into his hair and held his head to hers as they lost themselves in a consuming kiss. "That's it," he groaned, pulling back and inhaling unevenly. "I'm hooked."

"One kiss and you're hooked?" she teased.

"Maybe I can address the assembly about the dangers of addiction," he mused.

"Sure, and tell the kids what we discussed over breakfast. Don't even think of it," she muttered, her eyes glinting with humor. Her fingers floated to his ears, then behind them to his neck. "Tell me what you like, Nick," she begged him, suddenly solemn. "I want to please you too."

"You do."

She touched her lips to the hard angle of his jaw. "Tell me," she repeated.

His hands moved over her slender shoulders. "I like when you throw your arms around me and call me 'sweetheart,'" he murmured playfully.

She slid her arms beneath him, hugging him. "Yes, sweetheart," she obliged. He chuckled, but she remained serious. "What else?"

"Cecily—"

"Tell me," she insisted.

"I like your fancy underwear," he said, nodding towards the chair on which she'd tossed it.

"Do you want me to put it back on?" she asked.

"Don't you dare," he warned her, filling his hands with her naked breasts and sketching abstract patterns across the sensitive flesh.

As his fingers closed around her nipples she trembled, momentarily dazed by the searing current of longing that spun through her. She eased out of his grasp, determined to prove her love as he'd proven his last night. "Please, Nick," she whispered, struggling against the quaver in her voice. "Tell me what you like."

"I'll tell you in five and a half years," he joked.

"Now," she demanded stubbornly. "Tell me now."

He gazed at her, his eyes stunning in their dark resonance. "I like you touching me," he murmured.

"Where?"

"Everywhere."

She smiled slightly, then complied. Her hands journeyed down his sides, stroking his ribs, and then moved forward to conquer his chest. She ran her fingertips gingerly over his nipples, watching with blatant fascination as they stiffened into two tiny points. Sliding down the mattress, she directed her palms to his flat abdomen, feeling the convulsive tensing of his muscles there.

Her hands roamed to his hips, then his thighs. His legs were covered by fine dark hair, and she gently tugged at it, eliciting a breathless moan from him. His response to her touch thrilled her, exciting her as much as his touch had excited her the previous night.

She gathered one of his feet in her hands and massaged his instep. Phil used to love when she rubbed his feet, especially after a day during which he'd led his team in a vigorous workout or engaged in a spirited game of handball with one of his colleagues in the physical education department. But as her fingers skillfully kneaded Nick's ankles and toes, she thought not of Phil but only of Nick, pleasing him, arousing him, satisfying him.

Clearly she was succeeding. He groped for her arm and curled his fingers around it, pulling her towards him. She slid her hands back up his legs and covered his swollen flesh.

She felt his entire body lurch, as if a bolt of electricity had ripped through it. Her pulse raced with the sheer ecstasy of knowing what she was doing to Nick, knowing the harrowing joy she was bringing him. He writhed beneath her, shuddering as she increased the pressure of her fingers about him, nearly undermining his self-control.

With a throaty growl, he tore her hand from him and lifted her onto himself. Their bodies fused, and Cecily felt her own unleashed joy, her own wild response as he moved powerfully within her. He clung to her hips, holding her as he drove up into her, his body riding a forceful surge of untamed energy. She savored the building tension inside her, the compelling storm of passion that expanded with his every thrust, his every plaintive groan. Abruptly she felt it catapulting her into another world, a universe of indescribable sensation. She cried out at her arrival, her blissful defeat by the tempest of feeling that consumed her.

Nick followed close behind her, joining her in their own private heaven, celebrating their shattering instant of complete unity. Then he relaxed, his hands loosening their grip on her and rising to her waist. He held her immobile on top of himself, unwilling to release her."

"You were wrong," he whispered hoarsely once his chest had ceased its erratic pumping. "There *is* such a thing as perfection."

She nodded, her hair sweeping across his chest as her head moved against his shoulder. There was indeed such a thing as perfection; they had just experienced it together, and they could never again deny its existence.

She rolled off him, and he lifted the blanket over their cooling bodies. His face reflected his delight in her, his smile hypnotically sweet. "Actually," she mused softly, "it's your parents who are wrong."

"My parents?" He scowled. "How can you think of my parents at a time like this?"

"They're wrong if they don't think you deserve everything you've got," she maintained. "You do, Nick."

"Even without the official piece of paper?" he mocked, though his gaze was steady and sober.

"Even without," she swore. "How can they possibly think you don't?"

His eyes wandered over her face, and then his index finger trailed in their wake, tracing the faint hollow at her temple, the arch of her brow, the narrow bridge of her nose to its tip, the enticing curve of her lips. "I'm not the son of their dreams," he commented quietly.

"Maybe you're the man of my dreams," she countered. "I'll tell them that for you if you'd like."

He smiled briefly, then grazed her mouth with his. "They wouldn't believe you," he argued. "After all, you're just skin and bones. How can they trust a woman who hasn't even got pinchable cheeks?"

"I don't understand," Cecily remarked, returning to the subject. "How could you have disappointed them?"

He ruminated for several minutes, his eyes drifting past Cecily though his finger continued its quiet exploration of her face and throat. "They wanted a lot of kids, but it didn't happen. There was just Annie and me. Annie married Al right out of high school, and in a couple of years they had Bruce. But then Al was laid off for a while, and Annie had to go to work, and they never got around to having any more kids. I know that disappointed my folks. I don't think they cared so much about Annie's not going to college—she was a girl, after all."

"That's a terrible attitude," Cecily grumbled.

Nick shrugged. "They're old-fashioned people. They wanted their daughter to have kids and their son to go to college. But that didn't happen, either. They wanted me to be the first Faro to get a real education, *their* idea of an education, and it didn't happen. It doesn't matter what I've done with my life—they still haven't forgiven me for that."

"You could go to college now," Cecily suggested.

His eyes sharpened on her. "What for?"

"To get a real education," she answered.

"I *do* have a real education," he disputed her. "Not their idea, not yours, but mine." His lips cut a grim line across his face. "It bothers you, too, doesn't it?"

"No," she swiftly assured him. "At another time in my life it might have, but not anymore. Not now that I know you."

His mouth relented, shaping a pensive smile. He combed his fingers through her hair as he meditated. "Now they're doing it to Bruce, putting all their hopes in him, pressuring him to go to college and be the first of the family to get the degree. They were furious with me when I hired him on at O.R.—they said I was trying to corrupt him.''

"Corrupt him? For giving him an afterschool job?''

Nick ordered his thoughts before replying. ''He likes the work, and if he does decide to go to college he's probably going to need the money. But all these people are pressuring him—my folks, his parents, his teachers...''

Cecily felt a pang of remorse at the thought that she might be placing undue pressure on Bruce. But that was her job, and she shook off her guilt. ''Surely going to college isn't going to hurt him,'' she noted.

''Not if that's what he wants to do,'' Nick concurred. ''But honest to God, it's got to be *his* decision or it won't mean a thing. I'm the only person close to him who isn't turning his education into the issue of the century. The boy needs breathing room, and someone's got to give it to him.''

Cecily mulled over Nick's statement and nodded reluctantly. Maybe she ought to feel guilty for trying to push her student in one direction, the only direction that had ever seemed significant to her. She had wanted to go to college, and so she'd gone; but in retrospect, she realized that she'd never considered any other options. There had been no room for alternatives in her life plan; that was simply the way she'd been raised.

''I like Bruce,'' she announced.

''So do I,'' Nick concurred.

''I like him,'' she stressed, ''and I don't want to see him— or any of my other students—left with no choices at all. Nowadays you need a college degree even if your career goal is to sweep the streets. That's simply a fact of life.''

''You've got to say that,'' Nick pointed out. ''You're a teacher.''

"I'm a woman," Cecily refuted him, then grinned sheepishly. "I'm a human being and I care what happens to young people today." She weighed Nick's comments about Bruce and said, "You almost sound as if you honestly don't want him to go to college."

"Of course I want him to go, if that's what he wants," Nick defended himself.

"Are you sure you aren't just a little bit put off by the thought he'll be the first Faro to get the piece of paper?" she posed. "Are you—just maybe—afraid that he'll outclass you in the family?"

Her accusation, despite her tactful tone, struck a nerve. Nick withdrew from her, easing onto his back and staring at the rough-hewn ceiling above them. "I'm not in competition with him," he grunted.

She recalled his remarks about her husband, a teacher like herself, a man with the same educational pedigree she boasted. "Who are you in competition with, Nick?" she asked softly. "Phil?"

He twisted back to her, his gaze troubled, his jaw tense. "What the hell is that supposed to mean?"

"What you said before," she reminded him hesitantly. "By the lake, when you said you weren't like him." Nick opened his mouth to retort, but she touched her hand to his lips to silence him. "You *aren't* like him. He was no more of an egghead than I am, but he was a teacher and he believed in education the way I do. He had his collection of reputable degrees, and even if he was a jock he was a scholarly jock." She paused to sort her thoughts. "Of course you're different from him, Nick—you're different from anyone I've ever known before. That doesn't mean that I can't respect you, or love you."

The shadows marking his face dissipated as he accepted her reassurance. "I don't...I don't mean to compete with him," he swore haltingly. "But...You did love him. A lot."

"And now he's gone," she whispered. "I'll probably never stop loving him, Nick, but he's gone and I'm still here, living my life. You've lost lovers too, Nick. I don't know how I compare to them, but—"

"That's irrelevant," he interrupted. "There's no comparison."

"Of course not. There shouldn't be."

He digested her words, applying them to himself. A poignant smile whispered across his lips. "How did you get to be so smart?" he asked.

"Going to school?" she hazarded with a laugh. Her grin faded as she confronted him. "You're the smart one, Nick."

"How's that?"

"You knew...you knew right from the start that the last thing I wanted was pity. You knew exactly what I needed in my life, and you've given it to me."

"What did you need?" he asked with a derisive sniff. "An uneducated dunce?"

She ignored his self-disparaging remark. "I needed someone who could see that I was a woman. Not a widow, but a woman."

He studied her contemplatively. "The distinction I made was between being a teacher and a woman."

"It doesn't matter," she contended. "Either way, you figured out that I was a woman."

"It wasn't very difficult to figure that out," he chuckled. "Even for a dunce like me." He wrapped her in his arms and kissed her forehead. "It was pretty obvious, actually."

"Not to everyone," she claimed. "Only to someone as brilliant and perceptive as you."

His hands steered her mouth to his, and there was no more room for discussion. There was only the desire burning between them again, the desire of a woman for a man, the understanding of a brilliant, perceptive man for the passions of a vibrant, yearning woman. The understanding, the respect, the trust of two people who needed each other. That was what existed, what counted, what was most essential. They held each other, exulting in their understanding, enveloped by their mutual trust as the afternoon faded away.

Cecily ran into Gary Czymanski in the faculty parking lot Monday morning. "Your days of desperation are over," she crowed as he strolled with her to the school's door.

"Oh?"

"I've got you a third speaker for the assembly this Friday," she announced.

"Bless you, Cecily," he said, looping his arm around her and giving her a friendly squeeze. "I'm forever indebted to you."

"Hey, watch the hands," she scolded, wriggling free of his affectionate embrace. "Kids may be spying."

Gary scanned the vacant entry hall and laughed. "Shall I tell you what my wonderful wife Debbie thinks about career assemblies?" he bellowed, his voice echoing in the empty corridor. Cecily joined his laughter. "Who's the mystery speaker?"

"Nicholas Faro," she replied. "He runs O.R. Enterprises south of town, right near Glenville Industries on the river. It's a specialty firm that does trouble-shooting for large manufacturing companies. Nick founded the firm."

"I've heard of it," Gary said with a nod. "I've heard of him, too. As a matter of fact, he was invited to speak at career assemblies last year and the year before. He always turned us down."

"Maybe you didn't phrase the invitation properly," Cecily said with an impish grin.

"Let me guess," Gary murmured, stepping back to appraise her. "You offered him your body and he couldn't refuse."

She felt a blush crawl across her cheeks. "Gary," she whispered reproachfully.

He tilted his head, assessing her reaction to his joke. "You *did* offer him your body?" he guessed.

"We're...seeing each other, if that's what you want to know."

"Good for you," he cheered, slapping her heartily on the back. "Make sure you mention him in your classes. Get that student who's stuck on you out of your hair."

She laughed, thinking that she really ought to thank Richard Pettibone for having driven her into Nick's arms in the first place. "I remember the strategy, Gary," she managed. "Thanks for the advice."

Gary switched gears on her. "Seriously, Cecily—do talk up the assembly to your upperclassmen. Get them animated about it. We want the speakers to get a good reception."

"We certainly do," she affirmed, acutely conscious of Nick's reluctance to participate. She wanted the assembly to go smoothly for him. As confident as he was about himself, he still harbored some groundless insecurity about how others might view his lack of schooling, and she wanted him to recognize that he had nothing to be ashamed of on that account. "I'll definitely talk it up."

When she announced the upcoming assembly to her ten o'clock class of seniors, she tossed Bruce Munsey a discreet glance, curious to observe his reaction to the news that his uncle would be addressing his classmates at the assembly. He caught her eye and smiled meekly. She was relieved to see him grinning. Apparently he was willing to accept that his social studies teacher was a personal friend of his uncle's, and that her enthusiasm for Nick's professional success wasn't anything to be embarrassed about. As her gaze took in Bruce's large, athletic physique she recalled Annie's comment about how none of Bruce's fellow students would dare rag a boy with a build like her son's.

Her seniors, in general, met the news of the assembly with tolerant groans and jubilant remarks about getting to miss a couple of Friday afternoon classes in order to attend the presentation. Her juniors, however, greeted the news differently. Or at least one student did: Richard Pettibone. "You said one of the speakers is going to be Nick Faro?" he called out, surprising her. He rarely spoke without first politely raising his hand and waiting for her to call on him.

"That's right," she said steadily. "The other two speakers will be Dr. Michael Britten, a dentist, and Samantha Shepherd, a computer programmer at Glenville Central Bank."

"How come Nick Faro's gonna speak?" Richard persisted. "What does he do?"

"He runs an industrial business that he established himself," Cecily informed the entire class, avoiding Richard's disconcerting stare. "It's called O.R. Enterprises. Perhaps some of you have heard of it. Mr. Faro is a homegrown product of Glenville. He went to this high school himself."

"And then he started his own company?" a girl called out, clearly impressed. "Someone from this school?"

"That's right," Cecily confirmed. "I think you'll find his ideas interesting. Let's talk about the homework, now, shall we?" She proceeded, redirecting the class's attention to more immediate concerns.

She should have expected that Richard would be waiting for her outside her classroom, ten minutes after the final bell sounded and she'd packed up her briefcase. She took a deep breath to steel herself, then offered him a reserved smile. "Richard? Is there something you want to see me about?" she asked as she locked the classroom door.

He shuffled uneasily. She slipped her key into the pocket of her blazer and turned to him. One of his pale, slender hands combed nervously through his mop of hair. "About the homework, Mrs. Adams..." His voice trailed off.

Cecily suspected that he didn't want to discuss the homework with her. But his reluctance to reveal the true reason he'd been waiting for her didn't bother her. She'd just as soon keep their conversation focused on academic topics. "What about the homework?" she asked, starting towards the stairway.

He kept pace with her, tucking his textbooks beneath one arm and letting the other swing freely. "That stuff about constitutional monarchies," he began. "I mean, other than England, what are we supposed to look up?"

"Try the Netherlands," she instructed him. "Or Spain after Franco. Sweden. Greece. There are lots of democratic monarchies, Richard. I shouldn't have to tell you that. It's all in the book."

He mumbled something unintelligible. They reached the door leading to the faculty parking lot, and he quickly stepped ahead of her to hold it open. She nodded her thanks, and he accompanied her outside. "This career assembly," he ventured, finally broaching the subject Cecily knew he intended to discuss with her.

"Yes?"

"Well, what you said about your boyfriend..."

She flinched, then recovered. After all, she wanted Richard to know she had a boyfriend. "Yes?" she urged him. "What about my boyfriend?"

"Well...it's just, my nextdoor neighbor works at O.R., see, and..." He trailed off again.

"And what?"

"Well, see, I didn't realize when you introduced me to Mr. Faro that he was the same guy as my neighbor's boss."

Cecily's patience began to wear thin. She strode briskly toward her car, Richard keeping in step. "And?"

"And, well...I mean, from the things my neighbor said, well, I just didn't think that was the kind of boyfriend you'd have."

She drew to a halt and pivoted to face Richard. "Spit it out, Richard," she snapped. "What's on your mind?"

He nudged his toe against the asphalt, avoiding her flinty gaze. "It's just that you're always talking about how we should get good educations and all that, and, well, my neighbor says your boyfriend—I mean, his boss—isn't like that. Like, he never got an education. That's what my neighbor says. It's none of my business, of course," he hastily added.

That's right, it's not, Cecily muttered silently. "Nick Faro is an intelligent man who's taken an unusual route in his life," she said calmly, wondering whether other students would react like Richard when Nick spoke to them at the assembly. "What he'll be talking about is the risks and rewards of starting one's own business. He'll offer a slightly different perspective on things, and I think the students will be able to gain some useful insights from him."

Before Richard could question her further, they were interrupted by the low roar of a car approaching them. Cecily looked up to see Nick's red Porsche swinging into the lot and careening to a halt beside them. Nick leaned through his open window and shouted, "Hello, sweetheart!"

His timing wasn't great, considering the uncomfortable dialogue she'd been engaged in with Richard, but seeing Nick elated Cecily. Even his mischievous greeting didn't faze her. "What a surprise," she said impishly.

Nick winked at her, then turned to Richard. "How's it going, pal?" Before Richard could respond, Nick twisted back to Cecily. "I can't stay, *darling*, but I just thought I'd scoot by to remind you about what you said—"

Afraid that Nick was going to make some humiliating remark about their breakfast conversation, Cecily gave her head a nearly violent shake to ward him off. Teasing was one thing, but she couldn't have Nick making sly insinuations in front of Richard, especially not now.

Accurately reading her frown, Nick relented and winked again. "About dinner tonight," he concluded.

"What about dinner?" Cecily asked.

"I'll be late. I've got a meeting that might run over. So don't put the steaks on until I show up."

"What steaks?" She scowled in bewilderment. When Nick had dropped her off at her apartment yesterday, he'd vaguely mentioned something about their getting together for dinner Monday night, but they'd made no concrete plan.

"The steaks you promised to pick up at the store on your way home, *honey*," he said, his eyes nearly vanishing into two slits as he smiled. "Well, I've got to run. I'll see you when I see you, *baby*."

"Not *baby*!" she cried in dismay before convulsing with laughter. "Never, ever *baby*! I hate *baby*."

"Yes, ma'am," Nick obeyed. "I'll stick to pumpkin, all right? See you later." With that, he leaned back into his seat and tore out of the lot.

Richard stared at the retreating car and then at Cecily, utterly confused by the incomprehensible game she and Nick had been playing with each other. She was still laughing at Nick's incorrigible behavior when Richard spoke. "I guess...you and he really have something going, huh," he muttered glumly.

"Richard." She struggled to regain her poise. Her voice grew gentle as she studied her sudent's forlorn expression. "Surely I'm allowed to have a social life, even if I *am* a teacher. And you're allowed to have a social life too," she added meaningfully. "There are so many lovely girls in your class who'd be thrilled to have someone like you waiting for them after school, the way you sometimes wait for me. Take a look around, Richard. I think you'll see what I mean."

His eyes locked onto hers for a moment and he grinned meekly. "Yeah, well...maybe..." he grumbled evasively. But the sparkle in his eyes informed Cecily that, with Nick's exuberant and somewhat overbearing assistance, she'd finally driven the point home to her student that she wasn't the person he should be carrying a torch for.

She patted his arm affectionately, then headed across the lot to her Volkswagen. "I'll see you in class tomorrow, Richard." she called over her shoulder. "In the meantime, you look up Spain. And Sweden. Both excellent examples of a constitutional monarchy that works." With that, she climbed into her car and started her engine.

Her smile illuminated her entire face as she steered up Congdon Street, passing her apartment complex and driving directly to the supermarket. When she considered the love that had blossomed between Nick and her, having convinced Richard Pettibone to leave her alone was only a trivial side benefit of that relationship; but she was nonetheless gratified that she'd finaly gotten her message across to her infatuated student. He really was a nice boy, and she knew she'd grow to like him once he stopped pestering her.

She purchased two thick porterhouse steaks, some fresh green beans, and a bottle of burgundy. Then she went home. Not knowing when Nick would be arriving, she popped two potatoes in the oven, and then undressed herself and showered.

Nick arrived at her apartment earlier than she expected. Her hair was still wet from her shower when she answered the door, dressed in a snug-fitting pair of jeans and a turtleneck, her feet bare and a damp towel wrapped protectively around her shoulders. "I thought you said you'd be late," she remarked as he entered.

"Some greeting," he sulked, then grinned and kissed her. Drifting into the living room, he removed his leather jacket and kicked off his loafers. "I needed an excuse to show up at the schoolyard and badger you," he explained. "I had to invent something."

"In other words, you lied," she sniffed, stalking to the bathroom to hang up her towel and then sweeping past him into the kitchen. "I hope skillful lying isn't the sort of thing you're going to lecture the students on at the assembly Friday."

He watched her pierce the steaks with a fork and season them. "I don't know what I'm supposed to lecture them on," he commented. "Maybe you've got some ideas."

She rinsed the beans in the sink, then rummaged through her cabinets for her steamer. "Just tell them what starting your own business entailed," she advised him. "Tell them about how you recognized a need for your expertise and founded a company to answer that need. Tell them what it takes to be an entrepreneur. You know, capitalization, hiring, dealing with clients..."

"In twenty-five words or less?" he snorted.

Before she could comment on his sardonic tone, her telephone rang. Her hands were full of wet beans, and Nick answered for her. "Hello?" he said, then listened for a moment. "Sure, hang on." He extended the receiver to Cecily as she dried her hands. "It's for you."

"Who did you think it would be for?" she teased, taking the phone and lifting it to her ear. "Hello?"

"Cecily? It's Mom," said her mother.

She felt a fleeting touch of anxiety about Nick's having answered her mother's call, and she carried the receiver as far as its cord would extend, to the doorway leading into the living room. "Hello, Mom," she greeted her mother, glancing toward Nick. He had rolled up his sleeves and was arranging the steaks on a broiler pan.

"Who was that man?" her mother asked.

"He's a friend of mine," Cecily replied in an uninflected voice. "He's here for dinner."

"I see," said her mother. She fell silent for a moment, then informed her, "I tried calling you all weekend, but you never answered."

"I was out," Cecily noted.

Her mother momentarily fell silent again. "Cecily," she began falteringly, "I know you don't want us worrying about you, but honey...this weekend, well, we were afraid it would be a rough time for you. I mean, October 20th and all..."

"I know, Mom," Cecily said softly.

"Are you all right?"

"Yes," she assured her mother. "Friday was rough, but I'm really all right. Nick has been wonderful."

"Nick?"

"My friend. The man you talked to." She glanced at Nick again and found him searching her cabinets for wineglasses.

She knew he couldn't help overhearing her end of the conversation, but he was gamely trying to ignore it.

"Your friend," her mother murmured dubiously. "Cecily, I know you don't want me butting in, but honestly, honey—isn't it a little soon for you to be getting involved with someone new?"

"A little soon?" Cecily tried futilely to keep her voice clear of anger. "It's been two years, Mom. Which is beside the point. I met him, and we've become...friends. These things don't work on a timetable. They happen when they happen."

"That's true, of course that's true," her mother agreed rather too hastily. She hesitated before asking, "Are you in love with this man?"

"Yes."

Her mother sighed. "Oh, Cecily..."

Cecily's vexation got the better of her. "Mom, why can't you just be happy for me? Why are you acting this way?"

"Only because I worry about you," her mother answered earnestly. "This love affair seems—well, all right, it's not exactly sudden, but you've only just moved to Ohio, and you haven't even really been dating...I hate to think of you simply grasping at any man on the rebound. I just don't want you getting hurt, that's all."

"I've suffered the worst kind of hurt in the world," Cecily declared, her tone muted but resolute. "And I survived, and I've emerged all the stronger for it. You can't keep trying to protect me, Mom. I'm a grown-up, and I'm doing fine. If anything, you ought to realize by now that there are times when a person can get hurt and there's nothing her mother can do to prevent it. Things happen. Awful things. They hurt. But I'm still here, doing the best I can. Please be happy for me."

Her mother took a moment to digest Cecily's impassioned speech. "Of course I'm happy for you," she insisted. "What did you say his name was?"

"Nick Faro."

"Another teacher?"

"No, he runs a business in town," Cecily informed her, praying that her mother wouldn't ask too much about Nick's background. It would be just like her mother to ask where Nick had gone to college, and while Cecily didn't feel any compunction about telling her mother the truth about him, she didn't want to do it while he was within earshot.

Her mother spared her that possible awkwardness. "And he loves you too?" she asked.

"I think so."

"What—" Her mother's voice cracked slightly. "What do you want me to tell Phil's parents?"

Cecily sighed and fidgeted with the coils of the telephone cord. "Tell them the truth," she said. "Give them my regards and tell them I'll write soon." She'd always been fond of her in-laws, and since moving to Glenville, she continued dropping them a line whenever she could, updating them on her life.

"All right, Cecily. Don't be angry with me for worrying about you. I just don't want you to be doing anything rash. I'd hate for you to have to go through any more pain. You've had more than your share, and Dad and I can't help worrying about you. We both love you very much."

"I love you too," Cecily murmured, her eyes stinging with tears. "Take care, Mom—I'll be in touch."

As soon as her mother said good-bye, Cecily moved wearily back into the kitchen and dropped the receiver into its cradle. For several minutes she stared at the wall, batting the dampness from her eyes and trying to swallow the lump in her throat.

She felt Nick's hands curving over her shoulders. "Are you all right?" he asked quietly.

She nodded, breathing deeply, unsure of whether she could trust her voice.

He rotated her to face him and peered into her glistening eyes. "Maybe I shouldn't have answered," he said contritely.

She managed a feeble smile and shook her head. "Don't be silly. I was going to talk to her this week anyway, and tell her about you."

"What did she say that upset you?" he asked.

"It was nothing, really," Cecily muttered, reaching for a glass of wine and taking a long sip. The tart taste of it bolstered her, and her smile began to feel less forced. "My mother just has a way of making me feel guilty," she explained. "She says things that make me feel as if she doesn't approve of what I'm doing, as if she doubts my competence and my judgment, as if she thinks I'm still her little girl and I don't know what I'm doing. She doesn't come right out and say it, Nick, but that's what she's thinking."

He studied her thoughtfully, then nodded. "That's the way it is with parents sometimes." He succumbed to a bittersweet smile. "They don't have to live three blocks away. They can live hundreds of miles away and still interfere. Moving out of town doesn't always do the trick."

Her eyes met his, and she recalled what he'd told her about his own parents, about their disappointment in him even though the choices he'd made in his life were obviously the right ones. "Why do we let it bother us?" she asked. "Why don't we just go about our lives and not let them lay guilt trips on us?"

"Because we know they love us," he replied. "Because we love them too."

She set down her glass and crossed over to him. Nick's words proved to her the unique value of his own education, whatever that education had entailed. He was wise in matters that couldn't be taught in classrooms or in books, matters that couldn't be memorized like dates or reinforced with homework assignments. His wisdom was the sort that one could obtain only by observing, and by living.

She hugged him close, feeling his arms tighten about her, warming her, strengthening her. She could never feel guilty for loving Nick. She could feel only grateful, and incredibly lucky, to have someone in her life as wise as he was.

Eight

"I'm not going to stay tonight," Nick announced Thursday evening.

He set his empty glass on the floor of the terrace and slid his arm around Cecily's shoulders. It was almost too cool to be relaxing and enjoying after-dinner drinks outdoors, but the valley looked so lovely in the descending darkness that they couldn't resist dragging two chairs onto the terrace to enjoy the view. A glittering array of lights lay below them like scattered gems. Even Glenville Industries' smokestacks appeared benign, crowned with red warning lights that winked on and off in a tranquil rhythm.

Cecily and Nick had spent every night together so far that week, either at her apartment or at his house. His abrupt announcement that he planned to go home without her tonight took her by surprise. "Any particular reason?" she asked, placing her glass beside his on the deck and turning fully to him.

He shrugged. "I think I ought to spend the night trying to psych myself up for tomorrow's assembly."

"Psych yourself up?" She laughed. "Nick, it's not a Broadway opening. There's no need to get so worked up over it."

"I'm not worked up," he argued, then focused on the vista beyond the terrace's railing. His fingers wandered along the sleeve of her sweater to her hair and curled aimlessly through the auburn strands flowing down her arm. "How long am I supposed to talk for?"

"Ten, maybe fifteen minutes," she replied, nestling into his shoulder. The twilled wool of his blazer felt scratchy against her cheek, but she didn't mind. She didn't want him to risk catching cold by removing it. "Then the students will ask questions for another ten or fifteen minutes. And then you'll be off the hook."

"What kind of questions?" Nick asked, his eyes fixed on the fading horizon.

"How should I know?" she protested with a chuckle. "You've been to more of these assemblies than I have. What sort of questions did the kids used to ask then?"

"I don't know, I never paid attention," he admitted. "I was always sitting way in the back of the auditorium, doodling or dozing."

"Well," she mused, "I guess they'll ask about the things that matter to them: how much money do you earn, how big is your office, that sort of thing."

Nick grunted. "I'm not going to stand in front of a thousand kids and tell them how much money I earn," he objected.

Cecily laughed again. She was amused by the intensity and solemnity with which Nick was approaching the assembly. "You don't have to tell them how much money you earn," she reassured him. "Most of their questions will probably deal with your background, especially since yours is so similar to theirs."

His fingers paused against her upper arm, then toyed with the ends of her hair. He didn't look at her. "Am I supposed to answer them honestly?" he asked.

She twisted out of his embrace in order to see him. His eyes remained resolutely on the valley. "Why in the world wouldn't you want to answer them honestly?" she returned. "You aren't still worrying about your lack of a college degree, are you? For heaven's sake, Nick, you don't have to hide that from them. I think they're realistic enough to understand that to accomplish what you've accomplished in this day and age would require more formal education than you had. It's not going to influence them all to skip college."

"So you want me to tell the truth, then," he half asked.

"Of course I do."

"Even if—" He broke off and angled his face towards hers. "Even if I did some pretty dumb things in my past?"

She studied him in the light spilling through the glass doors from her living room. It etched shadows across his striking features, emphasizing his dark brows, the sharp line of his jaw, his long, straight nose. His teeth glinted where the lamplight glanced off their white surfaces. "What dumb things?" she asked, trying to read his enigmatic expression, wondering what on earth had him so apprehensive about addressing the students. "Were you in trouble with the law or something?"

He stared at her for a long moment. "Would it bother you if I had been?"

An undefined dread caused her stomach to clench. She reminded herself again that Nick's youth had been quite different from hers, and that whatever he'd done in his past, he had obviously developed into a mature, responsible citizen. Young people were entitled to make a few mistakes along the road to adulthood, as long as they learned from their mistakes and outgrew them.

But she couldn't quell her uneasiness. Lowering her eyes, she mumbled, "Yes, Nick, it would bother me."

He tucked his thumb beneath her chin and lifted her face to his. Smiling hesitantly, he shook his head. "Don't worry. I've never even gotten a speeding ticket in my life." Her eyes radiated her relief as he continued to examine her face. "Thank you for answering me honestly," he added. "If you'd said no I wouldn't have believed you."

What, then? she wondered. What awful thing might he have done in the past that would have him so concerned now? Maybe something had happened during his service in Vietnam. Cecily didn't personally know anyone other than Nick who'd served in that war, but she was aware that soldiers facing life-or-death situations were sometimes forced to make agonizing decisions. She honestly didn't want to hear about the atrocities Nick might have witnessed during the war, not unless it would make him feel better to talk them out.

But she couldn't imagine the students questioning him about his army experiences. To them, Vietnam was history, as distant from their own lives as the Revolutionary War. She doubted they'd be much interested in that.

"Tell me, Nick," she murmured. "What are you scared of? You're going to be fine tomorrow."

He forced a smile. "I just don't want to disappoint you, that's all."

"Nothing you could do or say would disappoint me, Nick," she assured him. She was as proud of him as he was of himself. He had achieved a near miracle in founding O.R., and she was certain that he knew it. "You're a wonderful man, and you'll give a wonderful talk."

"What if I'm boring?"

Was that what he was worried about? Did he fear that he might not be a dynamic speaker? Was he frightened that he might put his audience to sleep the way speakers had put him to sleep during his student days? She didn't believe Nick could ever be boring. The female half of his audience was certain to be transfixed by his handsome appearance, regardless of what he said, so he needn't panic about their attention flagging. And the boys would probably like him too. "You're going to be a hit," she declared decisively. "So stop worrying."

His lips flexed as he considered his words. "There are things about me you don't know," he said in a halting voice. "I..." He sighed. "I'm not a criminal, nothing like that. But...maybe I've done things you wouldn't approve of."

"That was the past," she commented gently. "All that matters between us is the present. And the future. You don't need my approval, Nick. Only your own. Whatever you've done in the past, the result is all right with me."

He bowed, touching his lips to hers. "I love you, Cecily," he murmured.

"I love you too."

Rising to his feet, he lifted the empty glasses and handed them to her. "I'd better get going," he said. "I've got a mirror at home waiting for me to rehearse in front of it."

"Lucky mirror," Cecily commented, leading Nick into the apartment.

"What's so lucky about it?" he asked as she carried the glasses to the sink. "It's going to have to watch me floundering in front of it, stammering and stumbling and making a fool of myself."

"Never," Cecily said with a laugh. "I'd love to be a mirror in your bedroom."

"Oh?"

"That way I'd get to watch you undress."

Her seductive comment caused him to grin. "Insatiable, aren't you."

"When it comes to you," she whispered frankly.

"Maybe I ought to give my talk tomorrow about the horrors of addiction," he teased. "I can drag you up on stage to illustrate my point. 'Here, boys and girls,'" he intoned, pointing a finger at Cecily, "'is an example of the ravages of addiction in action.'"

Her cheeks flaming with color, she shoved him towards the door. "If you're going, then go," she scolded him. She swung the door wide and gestured towards the stairway. "Goodbye!"

He grasped her wrist and brushed his lips against its inner flesh. "I think I'd rather stay here and watch you blush," he teased.

"I'm only blushing so you'll know I'm not perfect," she grumbled.

His smile faded slightly. "Nobody is, Cecily," he reminded her softly.

"Least of all, you. You've turned me into an addict. Now git!"

He stepped into the hallway and cast her a sly grin. "Do you want me to peddle my wares elsewhere while you go cold turkey?"

"You do and they'll be serving you in the school cafeteria for lunch tomorrow," she warned him. "Goodbye."

"Good night," he murmured, pivoting and strolling to the stairway.

Cecily watched until he was out of view, then shut and locked her door. She entered the kitchen and rinsed out the glasses, reflecting on Nick's nervousness about speaking at the assembly. In his position, he must frequently have to address groups of employees or clients. That wasn't the same thing as speaking before a captive audience of restless students, of course. Maybe he was simply edgy about returning to the high school after so many years away from the place.

It didn't matter. She was certain he'd be fine. He'd give a fabulous talk, and she'd have even more reason to be proud of him.

Her classes Friday morning went as well as could be expected, given that she was distracted by thoughts of the assembly. Fortunately, her afternoon classes were for juniors, which meant that they were cancelled so the students could attend the assembly. That meant that Cecily would be able to attend as well.

Just before two-thirty, she ducked into the faculty women's room to check her appearance. She didn't think she'd have a chance to meet with Nick before the assembly, but she wanted to look her best for him anyway. She adjusted the collar of her blouse beneath the lapel of her tweed blazer, then smoothed out her gray A-line skirt. A brisk brushing of her hair brought out its shimmering red highlights, and she applied a fresh layer of tawny gloss to her lips. Her quick appraisal of her reflection satisfied her, and she left the room and hurried directly to the auditorium on the ground floor.

Nearly all the seats in the cavernous hall were taken by noisy students when Cecily entered through a rear door. She spotted several teachers from the English department standing behind the final row of seats, and she edged down the narrow aisle to join them. After exchanging pleasantries with them, she turned her attention to the stage.

The stage's blue velvet curtains, worn and faded, were drawn shut. Gary Czymanski stood behind a scratched podium at the center of the apron, fidgeting with the attached microphone. He tapped it several times, recited a series of numbers, tapped it again, and called off-stage for someone to adjust the volume.

To his left were four metal folding chairs, three of them occupied. A stocky middle-aged man in a three-piece suit sat stiffly on the one nearest the podium. He fussed with his tie, then with the buttons of his vest. Next to him sat a petite woman with short dark hair, dressed in a stylish wool suit. Her hands were folded in her lap, her legs crossed at the ankle.

Cecily's gaze shifted to Nick and she smiled. He appeared the most relaxed of the three, slouching in his chair with one arm hooked casually over its back and one leg balanced perpendicularly across the other knee. The jacket of his pale gray suit was unbuttoned, his striped burgundy tie loosened, his crisp white shirt setting off his dark coloring in a remarkably appealing way. He leaned toward the woman beside him and whispered something. They both laughed.

Was this the same man who'd been so tense last night? Cecily stifled a chuckle. That was the way it was with stage-fright sometimes, she mused as she took in Nick's nonchalant demeanor. The night before, he might have been climbing the walls with sheer terror, but once he was on stage, all traces of his fear had vanished. She congratulated herself for having had faith in him when he'd seemed so unsure of himself yesterday.

At last Gary got the microphone to function, and he called the assembly to order. The din of voices subsided to a low hum. Cecily peered over the shoulders of two girls seated in front of her; they were bending their heads together and giggling. She recalled what Nick had told her about always taking a back-row seat at assemblies like this. She wondered whether the girls in front of her would manage to stay awake throughout the presentation.

Gary briefly outlined the purpose of the assembly and then introduced Dr. Britten. The stocky man in the three-piece suit rose and crossed to the podium as Gary took a seat beside Nick.

"My name is Dr. Michael Britten," the speaker repeated unnecessarily, "and I'm a dentist." He then embarked on a rambling description of the rigorous undergraduate and graduate training he'd undergone, his good fortune in being able to buy a flourishing dental practice in the Heights, the sublime pleasure he found in drilling teeth and fitting bridges. He talked for what felt like hours about techno-logical advances in dental office equipment. "When I first started practicing," he droned, "there was no such thing as a high-pressure water drill. You can't begin to imagine the torture those patients endured when I had to drill their teeth." His eyes glinted with delight as he said this; Cecily decided he must be a sadist.

He went on and on. Cecily glanced at the teacher beside her, who curled her lip. She caught a glimpse of the two girls in front of her playing "Hangman" on a sheet of looseleaf paper, covering it with inky gallows and letters. Then she focused on Nick, who was slouching even lower in his chair, trying futilely to appear interested. If this was what the as-semblies had been like during his school days, she could easily understand his snoozing through them.

Finally, Dr. Britten stuttered to a halt and invited ques-tions from the audience. "Do you use sweet air?" one rowdy boy shouted out. The question was greeted with cheers and whistles.

Dr. Britten didn't flinch. Instead he engaged in a long-winded monologue about drug therapy in dentistry. When he finished and asked for further questions, the students fell silent. Nobody wanted to risk giving him an opening for another verbose answer.

Gary diplomatically stood and hastened to the podium. "Thank you, Dr. Britten," he said, leading the students in lackluster applause. Once Dr. Britten was seated, Gary introduced Samantha Shepherd from Glenville Central Bank. The petite woman crossed to the podium and spent several minutes trying to bend the microphone to accommodate her diminutive height. The restive students jeered, and a few began stomping their feet rhythmically.

Ms. Shepherd took their gestures of impatience in stride. Once she started speaking, she proved to be much more interesting than Dr. Britten. She briefly mentioned taking a master's degree in computer science, but countered that by describing the many challenging computer jobs available to people with trade school certificates, which seemed far more attainable to many Glenville students than college diplomas. She explained in down-to-earth language what her job entailed, then opened the floor for questions. One student asked about "hacking," another about programming the bank's computers to play "Space Invaders." "That's possible," she allowed with an impish grin. "But mostly we've programmed the computers to play chess and a neat game of our own invention, which we've dubbed 'Looking for Mr. Spock.' This revelation was met with a burst of applause from the students.

After answering a few other questions, Ms. Shepherd stepped down from the podium, accompanied by more enthusiastic applause. A difficult act for Nick to follow, Cecily contemplated, but she had confidence in him.

"Our final speaker today," Gary introduced him, "is Nicholas Faro, who runs a firm in town called O.R. Enterprises. He founded this company himself a number of years ago, and he's built it into a very successful enterprise. I'm sure you'd all like to hear about how a Glenville boy made good in the industrial world. Mr. Faro?"

Nick nodded, stood, and moved in leisurely strides to the microphone. Cecily sensed not a flicker of nervousness in him as he readjusted the mike to his towering height. She heard one of the two girls in the front of her whisper to her friend, "He's *cute!*" and had to suppress the urge to vocalize her wholehearted agreement.

Nick offered a dazzling smile to the congregated students. "I don't know about this 'Glenville boy making good' stuff," he began. "It makes me feel like a returning hero or something. Coming back to Glenville High after all these years is a weird experience. It's funny how some things never change. I notice they still haven't fixed the water fountain in the lobby, and I hear tell they're still serving ground horsemeat in the cafeteria." The thunderous laughter that greeted this remark proved to Cecily that he'd won his audience over without any difficulty.

He proceeded to describe his company much as he'd described it to Cecily the first evening they'd spent with each other. He told the students what orphan drugs were, and pointed out the analogy between orphan drugs and what his company provided for industries in need. He mentioned the time he'd spent working for Glenville Industries, analyzing the problem the workers had with the machine that jammed in the heat, and deriving a solution. "It's kind of like, say, you're sitting in a classroom and there's a glare on the blackboard, so you can't read what the teacher's writing. Which may not bother you all that much, but for the sake of argument, let's assume it does," he said, casually combing a lock of hair from his brow with his hand. "Okay. The teacher doesn't know there's a problem, because she's up in the front of the room scribbling away. So you raise your hand and say, 'Hey, teach, there's a glare on the board.' Or, if you're a student like I was, you don't bother raising your hand. You just holler it out." The students chuckled. "Now in a classroom, you can do that because you and the boss are right there in the same room. In a big operation like Glenville Industries, the boss has his fancy office three buildings away, and he doesn't really give a damn if the workers are having a problem. And of course, in a classroom it doesn't cost any money to shut the blind and eliminate the glare, whereas at a joint like Glenville Industries, it's going to cost some major money to alleviate the problem of the jamming. It's because I worked at Glenville Industries that I learned about problems like this. And it's because I'm such a charming guy that I can convince the boss three buildings away that it is worth spending major money to correct the problem and make everybody happy. That's basically how it works."

"How much money do you make?" a student called out.

Nick's left eyebrow arched and he laughed. "Enough," he replied discreetly. "More than enough."

"Where'd you go to college?" someone else asked.

Nick hesitated momentarily, then bravely stated, "I didn't. My partner went to M.I.T. He has the technical training I lack. I bring to our company certain things that he doesn't have—a knowledge of what sorts of problems crop up on the line, an ability to relate to the workers, to comprehend their difficulties and to translate them into terms the bosses three buildings away can accept. I learned things working at Glenville Industries that nobody can learn at M.I.T."

He hesitated again, his gaze drifting from one side of the auditorium to the other, measuring his audience's attention. "Please understand that college is important. If I'd gotten a degree it would have been much easier for me to start up my firm. As it was, my partner was able to score other engineering jobs until O.R. was 'off and running.' I didn't have a degree, so I had to work nights washing dishes at a diner to make ends meet until we could capitalize and start pulling down salaries. I worked at Darlene's, off Chambers Street downtown. Any of you ever eat there?" At the chorus of affirmation which greeted him, Nick grinned. "Then you all know Alice, best waitress in town, right? Next time you go in there, you thank her for giving Nick Faro a job when Glenville Central Bank wouldn't let him in the front door." He winked at Samantha Shepherd, who chuckled appreciatively.

Cecily listened raptly to Nick. She'd never guessed that he'd worked as a dishwasher at Darlene's. That news made her recognize the hardships he'd endured in starting O.R. Her respect for him increased enormously as she considered how dedicated he must have been to accept such a menial job. That he would have done anything, even washing dishes at a diner, to support himself during those lean early years awed her. She'd never had to work so hard to reach her goals. Once again she was forced to confront the vast differences between her life and Nick's. But in the comparison, he seemed much nobler to her. She'd succeeded, but he'd succeeded against the odds, and that made his success far more valuable in her eyes.

"When did you graduate from Glenville High?" another boy piped up. His voice sounded suspiciously like Richard Pettibone's.

Nick's gaze circled the audience, finally locating Cecily in the shadowed rear of the room. She doubted he could see her enthusiastic smile, but his own smile faded as he scanned the room in search of his questioner. His fingers tightened around the edges of the podium. "I didn't," he answered bluntly. The room became very still for a long moment; the only sound in it was the constant purr of the ventilation system. Then the students began to whisper softly among themselves.

Nick must have misunderstood the question, Cecily thought as she stared at him. Or else he'd misstated his answer. Surely he didn't mean to imply that he didn't graduate from high school. But he silenced her confusion by repeating, "I didn't graduate from Glenville High. I never finished high school."

The whispering increased noticeably. Cecily glanced at Gary, who was sitting rigidly in his chair, his mouth agape. Her own jaw dropped and her head began to pound with the deafening drumming of her pulse. Nick, a dropout? Her Nick? It was one thing not to go to college, but not to finish high school....

She couldn't believe it. It seemed impossible. Everything she believed in, everything she'd built her life around—Nick had rejected it. As irrational as it was, she felt as if he'd rejected her.

"You dropped out of high school, and you're earning all that money?" a student bellowed.

Nick's expression was grim as he surveyed the crowd. "Look. I don't recommend that you try doing what I did. It was a stupid move. At the time it seemed like the right thing, but in retrospect, I realize I should have stuck it out. School can be boring, let's face it, and I was bored. I thought I could learn more out in the world than I could inside the classroom." He paused, his eyes shadowed with memory. "I could," he admitted. "I did. I learned some mean, nasty things. I learned that you've got to be twice as smart, work twice as hard, and struggle twice as long to be taken seriously. I learned—well, back in those days, I learned that if you weren't in school you weren't worth much else than to become cannon fodder in Vietnam. I learned that without a high school degree, you would end up with the lousiest, most tedious drudge work imaginable at Glenville Industries—if you were lucky enough to get a job at all. Today, they'd most likely laugh you right out of the personnel office if you didn't have a high school degree."

"Yeah," a girl shouted at him. "But you made it."

"It wasn't easy. In fact, it was damned hard. It would have been a hell of a lot easier to stay in school and get the official piece of paper. I made it the hardest way you can imagine, and I don't advocate it."

"You're telling us one thing," one student in the front row snorted skeptically, "but you're standing before us as living proof of the opposite."

For the first time since he took the microphone, Nick looked uneasy. He turned to Gary, who was still glaring at him, his face registering his outrage. Nick sighed and focused on the boy who'd made the remark. "I'm standing before you..." Nick spoke quietly, though his voice would have carried through the hushed room even without the mike's amplification. "I'm standing here before you to tell you that if you've got a dream, you owe it to yourself to follow through on it. That's the only message I've got for you today, kids. But for God's sake, don't make things any harder than they have to be. I did, and it cost me."

He swallowed, his gaze drifting about the room, alighting only briefly on Cecily and then darting away. His voice emerged, husky and constrained, when he spoke again. "Dream your dreams, kids. Build empires. Make Glenville a better place. But stay in school. There are teachers in this building, in this very room, who care about you. When I was a student, that was one thing I never knew. But I'm telling you: your teachers care. They want to give you every chance to see your dreams come true. Listen to them. Let them help you. You owe it to yourselves." He pressed his lips together, then exhaled, evidently fatigued. "That's all I've got to say," he concluded before stalking back to his chair.

Gary was still sitting in a dumbfounded state. The applause of the students jarred him, and he wove to the podium and made a few perfunctory closing remarks. Cecily didn't bother listening to them. She was in shock, and she raced to the door and out of the auditorium, eager to escape the pounding applause.

Eager to escape Nick, too, she acknowledged, as she leaned against the wall and tried to regain control of her frenzied nerves. She pressed her fingertips into her forehead, blinked, gulped several times. Somewhere in this mess there had to be some logic, something she could cling to.

All right, she tried to calm herself, all right. Nick was a successful businessman, intelligent, sensitive. He was a good man. She'd thought so as recently as this morning. Certainly the fact that he was a high-school dropout couldn't negate everything else.

But...a dropout! She couldn't bear it. His life suddenly came to represent the antithesis of everything she stood for: discipline, scholarship, the joy of learning.

Why hadn't he told her? Why had he kept such an important fact from her? She recalled his tension last night, and realized that he had probably wanted to tell her then. He'd said he might disappoint her, he'd said he'd done things she might not approve of. And she'd blabbered like an idiot that he could never disappoint her, and that all she cared about was the present and the future.

But that was because she'd never expected anything like this. A dropout! The very term was anathema to her.

"Cecily." Nick's voice broke through the dizzying whirl of her thoughts.

She peered up and saw him approaching her from the stage door. She felt a nauseating clutching in her stomach and spun away, once again anxious to escape him.

He easily caught her arm and held her in place. "You're mad at me," he guessed.

"Mad?" she choked. "Why on earth should I be mad at you?"

He stepped closer to her, refusing to let go of her arm. His nearness filled her with an unwanted warmth, and she stubbornly refused to look at him. "Last night," he reminded her, "you promised you wouldn't be disappointed."

"But—but I didn't know you were a dropout. A dropout, Nick! My God! Why didn't you tell me?"

He paused to assess her rage. "It was a long time ago," he noted.

"Sure," she snapped. "Sure. I went to high school once myself, Nick. I know how long ago it was. Everything I believe in, everything I'm trying to accomplish in my life, Nick—you turned your back on it. What means the most to me in the world—it means nothing to you. You walked away from it."

"A long time ago," he repeated. "I was a kid then, and I made a mistake."

"This is not simply a matter of making a mistake," she enunciated carefully, trying to contain her nausea. "I know you said we're different, but..." She bit her lip to silence herself as the auditorium door swung open and students began pouring out. She couldn't stand there, in full view of the student body, and argue with Nick.

He gripped her arm relentlessly, refusing to release her. "We're different, but what?" he prompted her.

"Not here," she muttered through gritted teeth, angling her head toward the students streaming out of the auditorium and milling in the corridor.

He scanned the hallway and tugged Cecily toward an empty classroom. Once he'd dragged her inside, he slammed shut the door and leaned against it. "We're different but what, Cecily?"

Too agitated to stand still, she paced along a row of desks, her arms folded across her chest. "But *this,* Nick, *this*...you haven't even got a high-school diploma, for crying out loud! If you'd stood up before that assembly and announced that God was dead, I wouldn't have been as horrified."

"How about if I stood up before the assembly and told them I had a criminal record?" he goaded her, his eyes burning with anger.

She raised her face to his. Panic underlined her delicate features. "You told me last night that you were never in trouble with the law," she whispered.

"I never was," he asserted, his voice a low growl. "But you're acting as if dropping out is the crime of the decade."

"It's not a crime," she conceded grittily. "But it goes against everything I believe in, just like committing a crime does. I have principles, Nick. One of those principles is that school matters, that it's important, that it's essential."

"And my life proves that sometimes maybe it's not essential?" he hazarded. "I'm living proof that some of us can survive without it? What's bothering you, Cecily? Do you think I dropped out just to prove that your life isn't worthwhile? What?"

She sagged against one of the desks and covered her face with her hands. "That's how I feel right now, Nick," she moaned. "That's how you make me feel."

"It's not why I did what I did," he said gently, daring to take a step toward her. "I once told you, if I'd had a teacher like you—"

"You would have gotten a crush on me," she retorted, recalling the conversation. "I don't care why you did what you did," she continued in a subdued voice. "That was the past. I'm talking about right now. I'm talking about what I believe in."

He tried to pull her hand from her face, but she turned brusquely away, staring at the window, refusing to look at him. "Last night you believed in me."

"Last night you should have told me about yourself," she rebuked him. "You could have prepared me, instead of dropping a bombshell at the assembly."

"I wanted to," he insisted, hesitantly touching her shoulder when she wouldn't turn to him. "I wanted to so badly, Cecily, but...but I was afraid. I was afraid you'd get all upset, and...and there you were, telling me you loved me.... I needed to hear you say you loved me, Cecily. I needed to hear you say I wouldn't disappoint you. I couldn't bring myself to tell you."

"Fine," she murmured brokenly. "Instead you told the world, and I got to listen in. Please go, Nick."

"Cecily. Don't be this way."

She was near tears, and she couldn't stand the thought that he'd see her cry. "Please, Nick," she begged him in a faltering voice. "Go away."

He didn't move for several moments. Then she heard his footsteps carrying him to the door. She listened to it creak on its hinges, then click shut. The finality of the sound shattered her control, and she cupped her hands to her face and surrendered to her tears.

Nine

Cecily ducked out of the school building and ran to her car. She didn't want to see Nick again, or Gary. Especially not Gary. Her mind filled with the image of his shocked expression when Nick had announced before the crowded auditorium that he'd never finished high school. Gary was undoubtedly furious with her for inviting a high-school dropout to speak at the assembly. She hoped that he'd cool off over the weekend and forgive her for her stupidity when he saw her on Monday.

She drove home in a blur of anguish. Trying to convince herself that times had changed since Nick was in school, and that a degree hadn't meant the same thing then that it did now, didn't help. She'd devoted her life to teaching young people, to persuading them to seek knowledge in books and classes and to experience the joy she herself felt merely by entering a school building. Nick personified the rejection of everything she stood for, everything she was trying to accomplish with her students.

Why did Richard Pettibone have to ask about Nick's graduation? she fumed. Why couldn't he have been his usual bashful self, too inhibited to verbalize such a question before an auditorium crowded with people? Recalling his cryptic remarks outside the school building on Monday, Cecily couldn't help suspecting that Richard had known the answer to his question before he asked it. He'd raised the issue only to humiliate Nick—and Cecily, the older woman who'd shunned his misplaced attentions.

But she couldn't really blame Richard. If he hadn't spoken up, she might never have known the truth about Nick.

How could she have given her heart to him? It wasn't that he had quit school; it was that he had hidden such an important fact from her. Of course, she would have been upset no matter when he would have told her about himself. But she was even more upset by the way she learned about it. Nick should have prepared her for this. He should have been honest with her right from the start.

She stormed into her apartment and slammed the door shut. Feeling a fresh lump of emotions swelling in her throat, she staggered to her bedroom. She threw herself across the bed and surrendered to a low sob.

She missed Phil. She wanted him. Wiping her eyes, she stood and crossed to the closet, where she found her wedding album. She brought it over to the bed and flopped onto the mattress, spreading the book open across her knees and seeking comfort in the photographs.

Phil had shared her ideals, she thought morosely as she examined the portrait of the radiant bride and groom before her. Phil had understood the true meaning of education. He had understood Cecily's goals, her dreams, her hopes for the young people she worked with. He had understood her passion for teaching, her desire to guide her students, her yearning to illuminate the world for them. That was what education was all about. Phil had understood that.

She inspected his face, his sloping eyes and easy smile. No. What Phil had understood was *school*. That was one kind of education, but not the only kind. Like Cecily, Phil had been educated in classrooms, in college and graduate school. Of course he had understood what was important to her; they'd lived such similar lives.

Nick hadn't. But that didn't mean he wasn't educated. Cecily hadn't been wrong in viewing him as intelligent. He'd learned his lessons just as she had. He'd followed his own course of study, pursued his own kind of knowledge, and scored stellar grades in the most difficult class of all, the class of life, of struggle and survival and victory. He didn't have traditional schooling, but he was educated. Cecily couldn't deny it.

She closed the album and ran her fingers over its white leather binding. She was seized by a memory of the night Nick had held her and consoled her when she'd been stricken by a relapse of grief. How kind he'd been, how sensitive to her. He'd offered her not pity but support. He was intelligent enough to make that distinction, and he'd given her what she needed that night.

It would be easier for her to understand Nick if he was more like her. But he wasn't. He'd lived a different life, been subject to a different environment. Cecily had no right to expect him to have emerged from his experiences with a viewpoint identical to hers. Her anger at him was born of complacency; she was refusing to accept that he could have made choices unlike hers and yet have emerged as wise as he was.

She forgot about eating dinner, showering, changing her clothes. She lay on the bed, watching the dusk darken her window as night dropped its blanket over Glenville. Nick was right: she was a snob. Not because she lived in the Heights, but because she was unwilling to judge him with an open mind.

He was a good man, a decent man. A smart man. He wasn't an egghead; but then, neither was she. It was irrational for her to feel as if he'd rejected her. They hadn't even known each other when he'd decided to leave school; and even if they had, he wouldn't have known her as a teacher. He'd have known her as a neighborhood girl a few years his junior, someone who spoke the party line about despising school and snuck a cigarette in the girl's lavatory every once in a while.

If she'd known him then, she would have known him simply as a dropout, and she'd have avoided him, missing out on a vital friendship. She'd have disdainfully viewed him as a loser, which was far from being the case. Nick was a winner.

She drifted into a fitful sleep and awoke, groggy and disoriented, late Saturday morning. Her bleary gaze fell to the wedding album beside her and she scowled. Phil was dead. He was gone. Her world had changed, and she had to change to accommodate it.

Standing, she returned the album to its closet shelf and shoved it out of sight. She yawned, stretched, and undressed, her frown deepening as she observed the creases sleep had pressed into her blazer and skirt. She hung the garments up and carried them to the bathroom, where she hooked the hanger over the shower curtain rod. Then she showered, filling the small room with steam and scrubbing the residue of sleep from her face and body.

The hot shower rejuvenated her, and her brain began to clear as she moved back to her bedroom and dressed in a pair of beige corduroy slacks and a turquoise sweater. After brushing the tangles from her hair, she ambled to the kitchen and brewed a pot of coffee. She filled a mug and carried it out to the terrace.

The morning was cool and overcast, and she wrapped her fingers about the cup to warm them. In the distance below her she could see cars feeding through the tall steel gates that opened onto the sprawling parking lots of Glenville Industries. The sight heartened her. Saturday shifts were a good thing for this town.

Two years ago, such a thought never would have occurred to her. She would have considered people who had to work on weekends unfortunate and put-upon. But living in Glenville had changed her perspective. Working a weekend shift was better than not working at all. Starting a new business and offering desperately needed employment to the town's residents was better yet. With people like Nick working to revive Glenville, it could once again become a thriving center for industry.

The problem wasn't whether he understood what was important to her. It was whether *she* understood what was important to *him*. She wanted to understand. She had to.

She reentered her apartment, rinsed her mug, and went to the bedroom to fetch her purse. Then she left the apartment and jogged down the stairs to her car.

She drove directly down the steep incline of Congdon Street, seeing her car's movement as a metaphor for her own emotional movement away from intellectual snobbishness to a more openminded view of the world. Cruising past Fisher's department store, she recalled the lingerie she'd purchased there and smiled. Downtown Glenville suddenly seemed beautiful in its homeliness, beautiful in the way that an elderly woman's face was beautiful, each wrinkle a mark of time's passage, a lovely souvenir of a rich life lived to the fullest.

Beyond the center of town, Cecily journeyed south and west to the train trestle. She switched off the car motor and climbed out, shivering slightly as an icy breeze gusted through the underpass. She picked her way carefully through the rubble, dodging a splintery heap of glass from shattered beer bottles, as she approached the graffiti-covered cement wall supporting the tracks. The paint sprayed across the concrete surface was fading and peeling, but Nick's initials endured.

Carving his initials into the unyielding stone was just the sort of thing he'd do, she mused. Painting might be easier, but he had chosen the hard way, seeking something of permanence. As he'd told the students yesterday, it was easier to stay in school and get the piece of paper. She didn't know why he'd chosen the harder path, but traveling it had hardened him as well, tempered him, strengthened him, made him the rare, fine man he was.

She still didn't understand his decision to abandon school, but she was determined to try. She climbed back into her car, turned on the engine, and drove to his house. It appeared empty, its windows dark, but she parked at the curb and strolled up the front walk to the door. She rang the bell and waited, then rang again.

After a while she realized that he wasn't home, but she circled the house anyway. She sighed glumly when she discovered his garage vacant. Still, she climbed the steps to his kitchen door and banged on it. No answer.

She trudged back to her car and slumped behind the wheel. She had to talk to him, had to try to find some common ground with him, had to hear his explanation. It was

vitally important. How dare he not be home when she
needed to see him?

She wondered where he might be. Perhaps he'd fled to his
cabin by the lake. Perhaps he'd been so hurt by her reaction yesterday that he'd run away, seeking solitude. She
considered driving to his cabin herself, but she knew she'd
never be able to find it. All she remembered about their trip
there was they'd driven past a bunch of farms, one looking
like another, and then into the woods. She'd be insane to try
to navigate blindly through such unfamiliar territory.

Sighing again, she ignited the engine and pulled away
from the curb. She coasted to the corner and turned it list-
lessly, slowing to a halt until a group of children playing
stickball in the gutter could clear out of her way. She inched
past them and turned another corner.

Two blocks ahead, she spotted a bright red Porsche
parked in a driveway. She knew at once that it had to be
Nick's; not many people in this neighborhood could afford
such a car. Gliding down the street, she realized that the
driveway was adjacent to his parents' house.

She shouldn't bother him while he was visiting his family, she remonstrated with herself. But her foot reflexively hit
the brake pedal as she veered to the curb before the house
and stopped.

Bruce Munsey was seated on the dilapidated front porch,
his arm slung around a slender dark-haired girl who Cecily
recognized as another Glenville High School student. She
vaguely recalled seeing them promenading down the school
halls together, arm in arm. Another student, a scruffy-
haired boy, emerged from the house and joined them. He
said something, and Bruce and his girl friend laughed.

Annie appeared in the open front door, holding a drink
and looking vivacious in a bright crimson dress. She spoke
to the youngsters, and then her gaze lifted to the blue

Volkswagen parked at the curb. Her eyes widened slightly, and she called over her shoulder into the house. Nick suddenly materialized beside her, clad in pressed khaki trousers and a pale blue shirt.

He hovered in the doorway for a long moment, staring at Cecily, his features set in an inscrutable mask. Then he edged past Annie, climbed over the teenagers' tangle of legs, and stepped off the porch to approach the car. Annie followed.

Cecily rolled down her window as Nick circled the car. "Hello," he said impassively.

She groped for something to say. Five minutes ago at his house, she was so sure of herself that she never gave a moment's thought to what she would say when she saw him. But now that he was beside her, leaning against her car and staring at her, she couldn't seem to get her lips to function.

Annie approached the car and grinned. "Cecily! Come on in, we're having a party!" she chirped.

Cecily swiftly shook her head. "No, I can't." Her eyes remained fixed on Nick's, searching for a clue to his thoughts.

"Sure you can," he said slowly.

"No, really, Nick—I don't want to intrude on your family uninvited."

"You've just been invited," he pointed out, his tone bland.

"Please come in," Annie blithely insisted. "Bruce just got accepted to Ohio State and we're celebrating."

"Oh!" Cecily smiled at the effervescent woman. "That's wonderful news, Annie. I'm very glad." She turned back to Nick. "Some other time, maybe?" she asked meekly.

Before he could speak, Annie declared, "You've got to join us, Cecily. Some of the credit belongs to you, after all."

Nick eyed his sister and then touched Cecily's arm. "Come on in," he whispered.

She caught a glimmer in his eyes, a glint of indecipherable emotion. His hand tightened slightly on her arm, and she conceded. "All right," she said.

He swung open the car door and helped her out. Annie raced ahead of them to the house to announce Cecily's arrival. When she and Nick reached the porch, Bruce smiled up at her. "Hello, Mrs. Adams," he politely greeted her. His two companions also smiled and nodded deferentially.

"I hear congratulations are in order," she praised Bruce.

"I guess so," he said, lowering his gaze modestly. "Thanks."

Nick ushered her into the house. An arched doorway opened from the front hall into a living room crammed with old but cozy furniture. Threadbare patches on the arms of the chairs and sofa were covered with faded lace antimacassars. The top of the television cabinet was covered with framed photos—one of Annie wearing a graduation cap and gown, one of her and Al posed in wedding attire, an informal one of Nick in an army uniform, leaning against a tree and grinning defiantly. The television set was tuned to a football game, and two more teenaged boys were sprawled on the floor in front of it, engrossed in the broadcast. Al was lounging on the sofa, and he smiled and waved at Cecily before turning back to the game. A tall man in his late middle age was seated in an arm chair, but he immediately stood as Cecily entered the room. His hair was thick and black, shot through with hints of silver, and his eyes were nearly identical to Nick's, dark and disarming in their intensity.

"Pop," Nick introduced her. "I'd like you to meet Cecily Adams. Cecily, my father."

The man gathered Cecily's hand in a crushing clasp. "It's a pleasure," he said offering a bright smile that uncannily resembled Nick's. He was, like his son, notably handsome, though his towering frame held perhaps twenty more pounds than his lanky son's.

"How do you do?" she responded courteously, flexing her fingers as sensation returned to them. She glanced at the television set and grinned. "Who's playing?" she asked.

"Ohio State," Nick's father answered, as if no other college team existed. "They're leading, ten-zip," he added boastfully.

An energetic woman bounced into the room with Annie. "Cecily Adams!" she boomed, drying her hands on a dish-towel. "Oh my goodness, what a surprise! Welcome, welcome to our home. I'm Nicholas's mother."

Cecily had expected Nick's mother to be plump, given his comments about how she'd view Cecily's slim figure. Mrs. Faro actually had a lovely figure herself. She was a bit shorter than Cecily, buxom, maybe a touch thick about her waist, with a soft round face and sparkling eyes. "I'm so glad to meet you," Cecily said earnestly, shaking the boisterous woman's hand.

"Nicholas." She confronted her son. "Why didn't you tell us Cecily was coming?" She denied him the opportunity of replying, turning back to Cecily and taking her hand again. "We've heard so much about you. Mostly from Annie," she said, casting Nick a reproachful look.

"Once a tattle-tale, always a tattle-tale," he muttered.

"Well, get Cecily a drink," she commanded her son. "You'll stay for lunch, won't you? It's almost on the table." Cecily opened her mouth to decline, but Mrs. Faro turned briskly from her and addressed the boys on the floor. "Billy? Jason? You having lunch with us?"

The boys peered up at her. "No thanks, Mrs. Faro," one of them spoke. "We figured we'd head off to Darlene's later."

"Hmm," she sniffed disapprovingly. "Stuff your faces with french fries and soda pop. It's a wonder you manage to stay alive. Nicholas, get Cecily a drink," she reminded him before marching from the room.

Cecily glanced at Nick, who was chuckling. "She's a terror," he warned her as he escorted her to the dining room. The table was already laid with dishes, an enormous bowl of salad, and several loaves of bread. At the sideboard, Nick mixed a scotch and soda for Cecily and handed it to her.

"I really shouldn't be here," she mumbled as she took the drink. "I didn't mean to barge in like this."

He gazed down at her contemplatively, his eyes resonant, although Cecily still couldn't translate their enigmatic light. "But here you are."

"I..." She sipped her drink and struggled with her thoughts. "I wanted to see you, Nick, but you weren't home. And then I saw your car here...But I didn't mean to interrupt a family affair."

"You haven't got a choice," Nick noted, rearranging two chairs on one side of the long, cluttered table so a place could be set for Cecily.

As if in confirmation, Mrs. Faro's voice bellowed from the kitchen. "Tony! Come get a chair for Cecily. Annie, go get Bruce and Melinda. See if Pete is eating with us or planning to fill up on junk at Darlene's with the others."

Cecily admitted to herself that, against a forceful woman like Mrs. Faro, she didn't have a choice at all. She obediently took her seat next to Nick as his father, Al, Annie, Bruce, and his girl friend trooped into the dining room. Mrs. Faro made a grand entrance carrying a huge platter of lasagna. She set it at the center of the table with as much fanfare as she could muster and then sat at the far end of the table, facing her husband. Still standing, he bowed his head to give grace. "Dear God, thank you for this feast Mama's made, and thank you also for getting Bruce into college and making us all so very proud of him. Amen." He raised his eyes and then his glass in a toast. "To Bruce. The first of our clan to make it."

"To Bruce," the family chorused, hoisting their glasses in his direction. He squirmed uncomfortably and stared at his plate, looking as if he wished he were anywhere but stuck in the middle of the family's effusive celebration.

The food was passed around the table. Cecily helped herself to a small portion of the lasagna, and Nick's mother intervened. "Take some more, Cecily," she directed her. "Look at you, you're all skin and bones."

Cecily shot Nick a quick glance and laughed. "I usually don't eat this much for dinner, let alone lunch," she objected.

"Nicholas, give her some more," Mrs. Faro overrode Cecily. "She eats like a bird. So do you," she nagged Bruce's girl friend. "Eat some more."

"Birds eat twice their weight every day," the pretty young girl remarked. "Isn't that right, Mrs. Adams?"

"You'll have to check with your science teacher about that," said Cecily. "But that's what I always told my mother when she complained about my eating like a bird. It's a good line, anyway."

The meal was festive, most of the conversation centering on Bruce, his plans for the following year, his expected success on the university's football team. Cecily watched him while she ate, trying to fathom his reaction to all the enthusiasm his college acceptance had generated. Was Nick correct to worry about him? she wondered. Was Bruce being pressured into something he honestly didn't want?

Thanks to the hearty appetites of the men at the table, most of the food was consumed. Nevertheless, Mrs. Faro made several indignant remarks about the meager leftovers. As she cleared the table, she scowled at Bruce's girl friend and muttered something on the order of the girl's having no flesh on her cheeks to pinch. "I've got a cake," she alerted the family. "So nobody move."

The mention of dessert was greeted by groans of protest even from the men. "Later," Mr. Faro countered his wife. "Let's digest the lasagna first, okay?"

Harrumphing, Mrs. Faro vanished with her daughter into the kitchen. "Nicholas, you'll scour the pan for me, won't you?" she requested.

"Of course," he complied. "You're on your own," he whispered to Cecily. "Go watch the game or something." He lifted the lasagna pan and disappeared into the kitchen.

Sated from all the food she'd eaten, and addled by having been unwittingly swept up in the family's festivities, Cecily took several deep breaths to clear her skull. She noticed Bruce and his girl friend standing in the living room doorway, watching the game on the television set. Cecily walked over and tapped his shoulder. "Can we talk?" she asked.

He immediately broke from his girl friend. "Sure, Mrs. Adams," he said.

She scanned the crowded living room. "Someplace private, maybe?" she suggested.

Bruce nodded and led her down the hall to the back door. They stepped outside onto a small rear porch, and the screen door clapped shut behind them.

Cecily gazed out at the tiny yard, where the grass was nearly invisible under a thick layer of dead leaves. She turned fully to the boy sharing the porch with her. "Bruce, are you happy about going to college?"

The question took him aback. "Of course," he said automatically.

"I know I'm your teacher, Bruce, but you don't have to say that if you don't mean it. Do you really want to go to O.S.U.?"

He frowned uncertainly. "Sure I do."

"Not for your parents, or your grandparents," she probed, "but for yourself?"

He chuckled. "Hey, I'm not going to pass up the opportunity to play for a school where the offense knows how to run a screen."

She briefly joined his laughter, then grew solemn again. "You know the odds are awfully slim for you to play pro ball after college," she reminded him.

He nodded. "Yeah, I know that, Mrs. Adams. But I figure, hey, I'll get a college degree out of it. I've seen my dad and my grandpa working at Glenville Industries all their lives, going from paycheck to paycheck and waiting for the pink slip. That's not for me. I want the chance to try something else." She was gratified to hear him say this. It proved to her that he was going to attend college for the right reasons. "I know I'm not the best student in the world." he continued realistically. "But I'm quitting my job at Uncle Nick's place so I can work harder on school. I don't want to fall behind when I get to college."

She nodded, pleased by his good sense. "What does Nick have to say about that?" she asked.

"He says if that's what Bruce wants, it's all right with him," Nick's voice emerged through the screen door.

Cecily jumped and spun around. Nick was lounging against the door frame, a tentative smile touching his lips as he observed the private conference. Cecily wondered how much he'd overheard.

He shoved open the screen door. "Your friends are about to take off for Darlene's," he told Bruce. "Why don't you go say good-bye to them?"

"Okay, Uncle Nick." Bruce darted through the open door, and Nick stepped out onto the porch. He stared at Cecily but said nothing.

"I wasn't saying those things to Bruce for your benefit," she murmured, reading in his unsettling gaze that he'd eavesdropped on the entire discussion she'd had with his nephew. "After seeing the way your family is reacting to his college acceptance, I realized that you were right in wanting to protect him from the pressure so he can make up his mind for himself."

"I think he has," Nick commented. He lifted his hand to her cheek and brushed a silky strand of hair from her face. "It's chilly out here," he observed. "Why don't we go inside?"

Inside was teeming with people, Cecily almost argued. She wanted to be alone with Nick, and she'd rather stand outside shivering on the porch than be swallowed up by his spirited family again.

He seemed to recognize her need to be alone with him. Taking her hand, he led her directly to the stairway. They climbed to the second floor, where he opened a door off the hallway and steered her ahead of himself over the threshold.

She knew at once that he'd brought her to his childhood bedroom. It was a minuscule cubicle, its one small window overlooking the gloomy alley separating his parents' house from the house next door. The bed was made, as Nick had once told her it would be, and the desk dusted. The shelves along one wall held several baseball trophies, also recently dusted. But what most astonished Cecily were framed certificates arranged on another wall. She moved closer to read them. One was from one of the town's grammar schools, citing Nick for academic excellence. Another denoted that he'd won first place in the town's scholastic science fair. A third marked his acceptance onto the junior high school honor roll, and a fourth labeled him "Scholar-Athlete" of his eighth-grade class.

Her mouth fell open. "Nick," she whispered, twisting around to face him.

He was resting against his desk, his legs extended before him and his arms crossed. He angled his head toward the wall. "Enough to make a teacher's heart soar, huh," he grunted sarcastically.

"Nick, you were obviously an outstanding student. What happened?"

He exhaled. "What happened was I was bored. What happened was I was smarter than half my teachers, and I was lightyears ahead of them, and they couldn't hold my interest. I was bored and restless, and all that the teachers seemed to care about was that I raised my hand before speaking and worked on my penmanship, that I knew how to stand in a straight line with my classmates and to always remember to ask permission before using the toilet. I was going crazy, Cecily. So I left. I figured I could learn more on my own than I could in such a stifling place."

She turned back to the wall, surveying the framed certificates and watching the pieces of Nick's life fall into place. He was the classic example of a gifted child, one whose teachers couldn't keep up with him and didn't try. Some school districts offered special enrichment programs for children like him, but Glenville didn't. The city lacked the funds to set up such programs now; evidently they'd lacked the funds when Nick was in school. So they'd concentrated their efforts on the slower students and left the most talented children like Nick to fend for themselves, or to slip through the cracks.

She didn't need a teaching degree to comprehend what had happened to him. But she did need a teaching degree to help students like him, students with their own individual talents and requirements. If Nick had grown up in her hometown, he would have profited from the many programs the school district provided for gifted children. But he had grown up in Glenville, where such programs were nonexistent.

"You see why my parents were so disappointed in me," he remarked wryly. "They had such high expectations. They couldn't understand why I'd throw it all away and go out on my own."

"I understand," she murmured, crossing the room to stand before him. "At least I'm trying to understand. School is so important to me, Nick, it means so much to me. Yesterday, when I heard you announce to a room full of kids—"

"I should have told you earlier," he cut her off, reaching for her hand and folding his fingers around it. "I should have told you right at the beginning. I should have told you the first time I looked into your eyes and realized I could fall for you. But I was a coward. I knew how important schooling was to you, and I figured you'd reject me as soon as you learned the truth. Which you did," he pointed out.

"Because I was in shock, Nick," she justified her behavior. "Because that was a terrible way to have to find out."

"Any way you found out would have been terrible," Nick commented. "Given where you're coming from."

"It doesn't matter where I'm coming from," Cecily whispered. "It only matters where I'm going." She lifted her eyes to him. "You're an incredible man, Nick, and I love you. That's another truth I've learned about you. I'll just have to accept you for what you are, Nick."

"Even without the piece of paper?" he asked.

"Loving you is more important than any piece of paper in the world," Cecily insisted.

His thumb stroked her knuckles as he gazed down at her. "Throw your arms around me," he implored her softly. "Call me sweetheart."

She circled her arms around his neck. "Sweetheart," she purred before kissing him.

His hands flattened against her back as he straightened up and drew her fully against him. His tongue met hers, then slid past it to reclaim her welcoming mouth. "I love you too," he groaned as he broke the kiss to catch his breath. "Even if you aren't perfect."

"What's not perfect about me?" Cecily protested.

He peered down at her and chuckled. "If you could see the color of your cheeks right now you'd know," he replied. Cecily felt them growing warm and hid her face against his shoulder. He ran his fingers gently through her hair and kissed the crown of her head. "You're just about as perfect as I could stand," he confessed, his words whispering down to her. "Do you think—?" He hesitated, his hands coming to rest on her shoulders.

She tilted her face up. "All the time," she answered playfully. "That's the way it is with teachers. We think."

He smiled briefly, then grew solemn. "How about the way it is with widows?" he inquired. "Do you think you'd ever be willing to give marriage another go-round?"

She gazed steadily at him. "I'm not a widow, Nick—I'm a woman," she reminded him softly.

He nodded. "I didn't have to finish high school to figure that out." His eyes wandered over her upturned face. "So how about the way it is with women? Do you think one woman of my acquaintance in Glenville would consider remarrying?"

Her smile deepened. "Only if the right dropout asked me."

"I'm asking," he said.

"I'm accepting."

He sighed in contentment, his eyes glowing blissfully, although he didn't smile. "You and I do know a thing or two about perfection, even if we aren't perfect," he reminded her seductively.

"And we'll learn a lot more about it," she promised. "It's part of life's education."

"The best kind of education there is." He gave her a final kiss, then relaxed his hold on her. "Let's go downstairs and make an announcement," he decided, as he swung open the door. "We can steal the spotlight from Bruce."

"Something tells me he'll be eternally grateful to us for that," Cecily predicted with a laugh as she followed Nick out of the room.

Take 4
Silhouette Special Edition novels
FREE...

and preview
future
books
in your
home for
15 days!

Start with 4 FREE books, yours to keep. Then, preview 6 brand-new Special Edition® novels—delivered right to your door every month—as soon as they are published.

When you decide to keep them, pay just $1.95 each ($2.50 each in Canada), *with no shipping, handling, or other additional charges of any kind!*

Romance *is* alive, well and flourishing in the moving love stories presented by Silhouette Special Edition. They'll awaken your desires, enliven your senses, and leave you tingling all over with excitement. In each romance-filled story you'll live and breathe the emotions of love and the satisfaction of romance triumphant.

You won't want to miss a single one of the heart-felt stories presented by Silhouette Special Edition; and when you take advantage of this special offer, you won't have to.

You'll also receive a FREE subscription to the Silhouette Books Newsletter as long as you remain a member. Each lively issue is filled with news on upcoming titles, interviews with your favorite authors, even their favorite recipes.

To become a home subscriber and receive your first 4 books FREE, fill out and mail the coupon today!

Silhouette Special Edition ®

Silhouette Books, 120 Brighton Rd., P.O. Box 5084, Clifton, NJ 07015-5084

Silhouette Desire

COMING NEXT MONTH

CAUTIOUS LOVER—Stephanie James
Jess Winter was a cautious lover, but Elly Trent knew there was
warmth locked beneath his controlled facade. Perhaps playing the
seductress would provide the key. . . .

WHEN SNOW MEETS FIRE—Christine Flynn
Life in the frozen beauty of the Aleutian islands was exactly what
Dr. Tory Richards needed, until things started to heat up when
steel-eyed Nick Spencer literally crashed into her world.

HEAVEN ON EARTH—Sandra Kleinschmit
When Samantha met Jason she felt as if she had stepped into a
romance novel. But when she learned that he was actually her
favorite romance author, fact became stranger than fiction.

NO MAN'S KISSES—Nora Powers
Hilary had always tried to avoid Justin Porter, but now a debt forced
her to work on his ranch. Could she prevent herself from falling
under his spell again?

THE SHADOW BETWEEN—Diana Stuart
The sale of the McLeod mansion drew Alida Drury and Justin
McLeod together in the game of intrigue and romance that
strangely echoed the past and cast shadows on the future.

NOTHING VENTURED—Suzanne Simms
Wisconsin librarian Mary Beth Williams took a gamble and headed
for Las Vegas in search of excitement. She found it when she met
Nick Durand and hit the jackpot of romance.

AVAILABLE NOW:

A MUCH NEEDED HOLIDAY
Joan Hohl

MOONLIGHT SERENADE
Laurel Evans

HERO AT LARGE
Aimée Martel

TEACHER'S PET
Ariel Berk

HOOK, LINE AND SINKER
Elaine Camp

LOVE BY PROXY
Diana Palmer